SUNRISE

ON

KUSATSU HARBOR

SUNRISE
ON
KUSATSU HARBOR

BY

DAN MALONEY

WINEPRESS WP PUBLISHING

WinePress Publishing (PO Box 428, Enumclaw, WA 98022) functions only as book publisher. As such, the ultimate design, content, editorial accuracy, and views expressed or implied in this work are those of the author.

ISBN 1-57921-858-X
Library of Congress Catalog Card Number: 2006903411

DEDICATION

This book is dedicated to my wife, Susan, and my daughters Meagan Bailey, Kristen Emily, and Lauren Elisabeth.

I'd also like to thank the following people for the spiritual, emotional, and musical inspiration they've provided me:

My grandparents, Nonnie and Poppie, (or Sue and Clyde Blackshere, as their friends called them) who taught me life lessons about love, caring, and hard work. My mother and father, Adrienna and Bill. My siblings, Donna, Debbie, Denise, Doug, and Dean. My high school English teacher Sally Miller, my football, basketball, and track coach, Leo Shaughnessy, and my high school government teacher, Mae Packan.

I'd also like to thank the following people who provided me with inspiration, encouragement and support: My cousin Betty White, Ruth Marcus, Elizabeth Kearns, John Brennan, Steve Arsenijevic, Andrew and Jenny Grover, Peyton and Michael Miller, Sharon and Gary Rhodes, Mario Lupia, Bernard Silverman, Jim Mahoney, Melissa Newton, Robert Paratore, Carrie Kyes, Lois Geller, Mark Cobb, Wayne and Karyl Palmer, Andrew Torres, Kim Currie, Terence Cotter, Reverend Irving Chase, Bob Adams, Michael Garlich, Dr. Barbara Volk, Albert Thomas, Barbara Hill, Reverend Charles Dougherty, Meg Goodman, Edward Murphy,

Tom Wesolek, Michael Newton, Carolyn Garlich, Kim Deremiah, Martin Retzer, Caroline Farnsworth, Reverend Clinton Roberts, Debbie Hyder Wilson, Jason Carson, Bob Hedstrom, Mary Winterfield, Bob Kutz, Reverend Cindy Karis, Jon Matousek, Luke Ivers, Patrick Sweeney, and "Wild" Bill Nienow.

Musical artists Stephen Bishop, Neil Young, Supertramp, Crosby, Stills & Nash, Santana, Bruce Springsteen, Joni Mitchell, James Taylor, Phil Collins and Genesis, Tracy Chapman, Jesse Colin Young, Jackson Browne, Laura Nyro, Carole King, Art Garfunkel, Parker McGee, The Beatles, Kenny Loggins, Frank Sinatra, Tony Bennett, Hall and Oates, Ricki Lee Jones, Jimmy Webb, John Mayer, Sarah McLachlan, Dar Williams, Stevie Wonder, Peter, Paul, and Mary, John Prine, Steve Goodman, and Eric Carmen.

Authors J.D. Salinger, Ayn Rand, Leo Buscaglia, Don Hutson, Jim Rohn, Gary Larson, and Jim Unger. Former fellow employees Mitch, Danny, Neal, Joe, Tommy and the whole third shift.

A special thank you to Susan Bono, my first draft editor.

My original goal for writing this story was to provide my daughters with a lesson in character. I hope I've succeeded.

And, of course, my thanks to God, because, as much as I would like to claim that I wrote this story by myself, I'll always believe that the ideas in this book came from a power greater than me.

This entire story is a work of fiction.

FIRST EDITION ACKNOWLEDGEMENTS

Without the commitment from the following people, this story would never have been published. They took the time to read and understand the message of hope this story conveys and then agreed to allow this unknown author to test market his story in their establishments. Their commitment to this story is as much a part of the story as Mieko and Tori. Thanks to all of you and here's hoping that the message that spreads through your doors will open up more around the country.

I'd also like to thank Athena Dean and all of the wonderful people at Winepress Publishing who helped me on this journey.

—Dan Davis Maloney

From Naperville, Illinois

Gail Andrews—The Canterbury Shoppe
Cheryl Wieczorek, Denise Provenzano—Zano Salons
Susan Chanin—Egg Harbor Cafe
Andrea Clark, Mary Ellen Anderson—Bee Entertaining
Bill Anderson—Oswald's Pharmacy
Bob Johnson—Innovations Salons

Evelyn Barsh—Lori's Designer Shoes
Elden DeJarnett—Winestyles
Dolly Long, Lori Sprovier—Simply Hair Salons
Gloria White—Butterfield's Café
Ann Solomon—Country Curtains
Lisa Sallstrom—Jon Ric Salon
Debbie Hennen—Deborah Jean's Apparel
Joe Weston—Crème de la Crumb Café
Loretta Wilger-Asmus—Looks Salon
Kristin Guill—The Heritage Shoppe
Grace Song—Naperville Florist
Gary Chomko—Curves for Women
Marian Kraus—L'Artiste[2]

La Jolla, California

Rhana Pytell—Gaia Day Spa
Aurel—Aurel Salon
Ann Paliotti—From My Garden Gift Shop

Southampton, New York

Debbie Cirruzzo—La Carezza Day Spa
Pamela Ornstein—Ananas Spa

"Look back on your life's path and you will find that the fears you once had look much different now than when you faced them for the first time. As we take this journey into the unknown, resolve to live without fear, as today is only a perception subject to change."

—Dan Davis Maloney

Chapter 1

I have always loved my wife.

We celebrated our eighteenth wedding anniversary two months ago. We were fortunate to meet at work and fall in love when we did. We were blessed with three beautiful daughters and, although we never had a lot of material possessions or saved much money, we always had a great deal of love in our home.

Like most couples, we worked through our share of troubles and trying times, but we always maintained our commitment to each other. Our love was the glue that held us together. I tell you this because I have a true story to tell about a couple of people who also made a commitment to one another. It's like no story you have ever heard.

I'm not a writer by profession, but some recent events have transpired that make it necessary for me to finally tell this story. If I wait any longer, I fear it will never be told. I know in my heart that it is far more important for my children and grandchildren that this story be told than to worry about how it is written.

I know you will understand when you finish.

DISCOVERY

Several years ago my wife and I hopped into our car on a sunny Saturday morning and, with the classifieds from the newspaper in hand, began a day of garage sale shopping. We didn't have much money back then, but once a month we would find a way to scrape together about twenty-five dollars. Then we'd set out to find some bargains at the local garage sales.

We both enjoyed antiques and, like many antique treasure hunters, were always hoping to find a diamond in the rough at some estate sale. The closest we ever came to discovering a hidden treasure was in early June of 1979 when we spotted a brown vase at a garage sale in the town of Auburn, California. The color and design of the vase made me believe that it was crafted by an Indian. I wanted to buy it. I believed it would add some Native American flavor to our family room. The price was only two dollars and fifty cents.

I can still remember that short conversation with my wife as if it were yesterday. My persuasive abilities were put to the test.

"Honey," I said, "I really think this would look great in the family room next to the bookshelves."

"Over my dead body," she replied.

I ended up buying it, but it just gathered dust in the attic until several years later when we took the vase to a benefit antique show at the local high school. I gave one of those traveling appraisers a five-dollar donation to tell us about it. He told us it was a ceremonial urn from the Shasta Indian tribe, one of the many tribes that had long since disappeared from our region. He also said it was worth at least five hundred dollars.

I can't tell you my wife liked it any better after we discovered its value, but today it's filled with eucalyptus and sits in our family room next to our antique icebox.

On that Saturday morning in early January of 1981, we were about five miles from home when we came to a garage sale of an individual who had moved out of the country a few months earlier. He had left his small house for the realtors to sell. He had not wanted to transport all of his belongings overseas, and consequently left much of his furniture and many dishes and appliances.

Most of the furniture was old, including a few heavily-upholstered chairs. We considered buying them until I spotted some makeshift repairs that had damaged their frames.

We became excited when we saw a small oak kitchen table we desperately needed. It had one broken leg that I knew could easily be repaired. We purchased the table for twenty-two dollars and were lugging it back to the car when I spotted a cardboard box packed full of used videocassette tapes. After we loaded the table into the car, I went back and looked through the box of tapes.

My parents had given us a VCR the previous Christmas, and like most blue-collar working folks, we couldn't afford to buy new movies. We were always thrilled when we were able to find used videotapes at garage sale prices. Oftentimes we could buy a tape for less than the rental cost at the video store.

Since receiving our VCR, we made it a point to try to have a family movie night at least one Saturday night each month. It was one of our favorite regular family events. We would get a large bowl of popcorn and sit together on our old sofa to watch a favorite movie.

Most of our movies were musicals, because my three daughters loved to sing and dance. I'm sure they knew every song and dance from *Seven Brides for Seven Brothers, Brigadoon, and My Fair Lady*. It was always fun to watch our girls reenact the movies and argue about who would have to play the boys' parts.

The one great musical we did not own was *The Sound of Music*. My girls loved that movie. They watched it every Easter when it aired on television. At the garage sale that day, I found a tape marked *The Sound of Music*. I didn't tell my wife. I secretly paid the attendant for the movie and slid it into my jacket. I thought I was going to be a hero.

The following Saturday night I told my daughters that I had a special surprise for them. We prepared the popcorn and gathered around the TV. I popped the videotape into the VCR, and when the opening credits appeared they all let out piercing squeals of delight.

My wife gave me a warm smile and squeezed my hand. What happened next changed everyone's lives. When Julie Andrews finished the opening title song and began her run down the mountain to the abbey, the movie suddenly came to an abrupt halt.

On the screen before our eyes was an old Japanese gentleman sitting in one of the chairs we had seen at the garage sale the previous week. I recognized the man as a former co-worker from the factory where I worked. He had retired a few months earlier because of a heart condition.

His name was Mieko and what follows is an incredible story that he told us on that videotape. I've done my best to piece together as much of the detail as possible from his narration. His story has changed my life.

Chapter 3

MIEKO'S STORY

Mieko Takachi grew up about two miles from Kusatsu Harbor, one of the many bustling ports in southern Japan. His family consisted of his mother, father, grandfather, and two brothers. Mieko's parents raised him, their oldest son, to understand that one day he would be the head of his family.

His parents provided him with tutors at a young age after they discovered he was blessed with a prodigious gift for understanding the sciences. From the age of nine, Mieko was the most promising student in his school. At the age of fourteen he attended classes at the local medical school.

Mieko grew taller than most of his friends, standing almost six feet tall. He wore glasses from the age of twelve, and although he looked bookish, he developed into one of the strongest boys in his neighborhood.

He learned patience while working on his father's fishing boat and never hesitated tackling the most difficult job when it was necessary. He loved challenges.

On his eighteenth birthday his grandfather met him down by the boat docks and took him aside to give him some advice.

"Mieko," he said, "Now that you are getting older, you must remember that above all things in life, your family must always come first. Employers will want you to work your fingers to the bone for their benefit. They do not care about your family."

His grandfather sat down on a weathered gray wooden bench.

"Now that we are at war, our country will want you to fight to your death to protect our homeland. All these things are important, but none so much as protecting and defending your family. Without family, you are like a leaf blowing in the wind. I have seen you with Tori and I know that someday you will marry her and have a family of your own. Always remember to live your life for your family and you will live happily."

Mieko listened carefully. It was the first time his grandfather had spoken to him in such a manner. Mieko knew that his grandfather was right about one thing. Any day now the government would be asking him to fight in the war.

It was December 1944, World War II had engulfed their country, and the only thing that prevented Mieko from having been called earlier to serve as a soldier was the work he was doing in the hospital laboratories. His medical skills enabled him to become part of a select group of scientists. They worked on ways to stop infections from spreading in those who had been wounded in the war. His job was to find a way to keep men alive longer so that they could continue the fight. But Japan had incurred many losses and more and more men were being taken from the laboratories to fill the ranks. Mieko knew his research was ending and he would be called soon to serve.

Mieko was surprised when his grandfather mentioned Tori. Mieko never realized his feelings for Tori were so obvious to others.

Tori grew up next door to Mieko and, from the time they were able to walk, they had been good friends. Tori held an inner strength and a kind heart. She was one year younger than Mieko, but the oldest of five sisters and two brothers.[1]

In the summer of 1939, at the age of twelve, Tori's life changed. Her Aunt Shurei came from California to live with the family. Aunt Shurei was a converted Christian. She taught Christianity and English to Tori and the neighbors for the next two years while she prepared to move to Africa, where she lived as a missionary until she was killed in an uprising in 1943. Tori listened to the stories of the power of prayer and forgiveness. Both Tori and Mieko listened to her aunt's stories of living in San Francisco with people of all cultures. Tori's family converted to Christianity, and Tori's own beliefs grew stronger one day, late in that summer, when she accompanied her father on a fishing trip.

Mieko's father, Masao, was a fisherman, making the trip each day out to net fish for the local markets. He'd lost his left arm in a Pacific battle a year earlier and returned home to become a fish supplier to the army and local civilian markets. His was one of the few boats still being permitted to go out for deep-sea fishing. Most of the other boats had been taken over by the army and fitted with weaponry. That week several of his crew had fallen ill. He asked Tori's father, Shigeru, to help him for a few days aboard his boat. Shigeru's sight, failing in the past three years from developing cataracts, prevented him from serving in the army, but he still maintained his physical strength and could help lift the nets. Shigeru previously made his living as an auto mechanic spending his days repairing army trucks for the local transportation depot. Recently the depot cut back their workforce and Shigeru was left to spend his time repairing bicycles and a few automobiles at a local repair shop.

When Tori heard that her father was going out with Masao for the day, she asked if she could go.

---

[1] Author's note: Mieko became tearful with almost every mention of Tori, necessitating occasional long pauses during his telling of the story. We would learn the reason and understand later.

"May I come and watch? I'll stay out of the way. I've never been on a boat. Please."

"It's not a place for a young girl," he told her. She turned, put her head down, and started to walk away. Shigeru watched her and then relented. "All right, you can come, but you have to stay out of the way. There is a lot of work to do on a fishing boat and I don't want to have to worry about you." Shigeru knew Tori would behave. She was his favorite child and he saw no harm in letting her spend the day watching from the deck.

Tori beamed. She turned and ran into Shigeru's arms.

"Thank you, thank you, I'll stay out of the way, I promise." She gave him a kiss on the cheek.

The next morning she followed her father to the boat. Tori watched as Mieko and the men worked all day, pulling up nets of tuna, halibut, and other fish and loading them into the hold. They turned to head back to the harbor earlier than usual and Masao walked over to Tori as they were leaving the fishing grounds. He smiled as he handed her a fish.

"Take this home and make your family a nice dinner tonight. I think you brought us good luck today. We haven't caught this many fish in months. Our hold is almost full." He spoke to Tori and her father. "You'll always be welcome on my boat."

"Thank you," Tori said taking the fish in her hands, "but I'm feeling a little ill."

"Just a little seasickness," her father said. "Tori, if you need to, just lean over the rail and relieve yourself. We all do sometimes."

As they made their way back into the harbor, Tori felt the urge and leaned over the rail, still holding the fish that was given to her. Suddenly the fish slipped out of her hands and she instinctively dove forward to grab it and lost her balance. Her legs shot up into the air as she grabbed the rail with one hand and dangled over the side of the boat. Her father scrambled to reach her, but as he reached out to grasp her hand it slipped off the rail and she fell into the sea. She became entangled in the nets that had not yet been hoisted. She fought hard to escape the netting, but the harder she fought, the more entangled she became. It would only be a matter of minutes before she would drown.

Up on deck Masao started yelling directions to everyone and Shigeru prepared to jump in to save her, but realized he, too, would get caught up in the nets. He paused for a moment, and before he could make another move, he saw Mieko moving quickly to grab the net swing handles. With all of his strength, Mieko raised the framed netting above the water and held it steady as the water drained from the netting. Tori was able to breathe again. Then Mieko and Masao worked together to swing the heavy nets around and dropped Tori and hundreds of flopping fish onto the deck.

As she lay in the midst of the piles of fish, she turned to her father, Shigeru.

"Father, I prayed to God when I was underwater. I prayed that I would see you again. A voice told me Mieko would save me. God led Mieko to save me."

The men looked at one another, unconvinced that God had anything to do with saving Tori. Shigeru hugged Tori, then turned and shook Mieko's hand.

"Thank you for saving my daughter. She means everything in the world to me. I don't know what I would have done if I'd lost her."

Tori flashed a smile at Mieko. He smiled back.

When they got back to port, Mieko walked Tori home. They grew closer to each other after that day. Over time they became the closest of friends. It was during the next few years that their love developed. Mieko couldn't remember exactly when it was they fell in love, or if there actually ever was a turning point. They just grew closer with each passing year.

Tori grew into a beautiful young woman. Her features were delicate, and she only grew to four feet and ten inches. Mieko always compared her to the butterflies in the fields. She brought a gentleness of spirit to everyone she met and a beauty to all that surrounded her. She always seemed to be smiling. At school she was one of the most-liked students in her class. At home she learned cooking, sewing, and gardening from her mother, important skills for a wife in Japanese society. Tori was sensitive to others' feelings and never hesitated to help anyone in need.

Since the beginning of the war, when Mieko was fifteen and Tori was fourteen, they would start their day by walking down to Kusatsu Harbor and saying prayers for all of the men at war. They discovered a remote area of the harbor that was hidden from view by several large boulders. They devoted the first hour of each day, before Mieko had to report for work, to sitting and talking at the harbor. It became their personal refuge from the rest of the world at war.

They watched the boats from all over the world come in and out of the harbor. As they grew older they began to talk of marriage plans and how they would sail away on a trip one day after the war.

Each morning at the harbor brought memories that would last forever. The clanging bells and shrill whistles of the boats would bring life to the port each morning. Fishing boats sailed out of the harbor and screeching gulls would follow, gliding on the breezes as if they were kites attached to the vessels by invisible wires.

Most mornings Mieko and Tori arrived in time to see a magnificent sunrise over Kusatsu Harbor. When they were together, all the sunrises were magnificent. Sometimes they would talk for the entire hour. Sometimes they would say barely a word and just hold hands. Occasionally Mieko whistled tunes that he made up and Tori laughed at his attempts to be a musician.

"Mieko, stick to your sciences," she told him. "You'll never be a musician."

Mieko laughed at her, agreeing that he would never make a living as a musician. One day he surprised her.

"Tori, I've made up a special tune for you and named it '*The Harbor Song*' in honor of our favorite spot."

She listened to it and applauded his efforts.

"Maybe I spoke too soon." Tori tried whistling the tune back to Mieko. She made it sound even better. "I like it," she told him. "That's a song even the birds would love. Maybe you can play it at our wedding."

They spent the rest of that hour laughing and whistling variations of "*The Harbor Song*." They continued to whistle it all the way home.

Two weeks after his eighteenth birthday Mieko received the letter he had been expecting. The next morning, as they stood at the boulders, Mieko held Tori's hand and gave her the news.

"I've finally been called to serve in the army. I am to report to Urakami prison the day after tomorrow for duty. I guess they must have a training camp there. I can only promise that I'll do what I can to end this war as soon as possible and come back to you." He looked into Tori's eyes and told her what she always hoped to hear. "You know, Tori, I will always love you and only you. Your beauty will always give me inspiration. I will think of you every day until I return." Mieko gently caressed her hair. "Please keep coming down here to the harbor and saying prayers for me each morning. Whatever happens, wait for me. I promise to never love anyone but you."

Tori could not hide her tears. No one could predict what would happen from this day forward. Many other events would dictate the shape and course of their lives. She knew Mieko could get killed. Tori cried on his shoulder as they walked back to their homes.

As he was about to leave her, she looked up with tears streaming down her face.

"Wait here," she said. She ran inside and grabbed a small wooden box from under her pillow. She returned and held Mieko's face in her hands. She looked up at him and stared into his eyes. "I will never love anyone but you. My thoughts will be with you every day. Come back to me soon. I will be here waiting for you." She opened the box and pulled out a small gold medallion on a chain. Tori took Mieko's hand in hers and placed the medallion in his palm. She looked at him and said, "What do you see on this medallion?"

Mieko raised it to his eyes and looked closely. The medallion was old and worn.

"It looks like a man, a robed warrior, with a bow slung over his shoulder, looking at a sunrise."

Tori smiled.

"My grandmother gave that to me. She told me it belonged to our ancestor, a great samurai warrior many years ago." She looked into Mieko's eyes. "My grandmother told me once that I would be able to judge any man's character by whether the man believed the sun was rising or setting. If he believed it to be rising, he was a hopeful and optimistic man whom I should consider marrying. But if the man saw a setting sun, I should avoid him, as he would always believe that life was difficult and unyielding. Take it and think of me."

When Mieko looked at the medallion he could not imagine how anyone could see anything but a rising sun. He put the medallion around his neck and vowed he would wear it as a reminder of their love.

That evening Mieko sat with his family.

"Grandfather, you have told me what family means. Father, you have taught me patience. I vow to you that I will use everything you've both taught me to help Japan win this war and come back here to our family. I will help get our lives back to where they were before all this started. I will make you all proud."

He fell asleep that night thinking it strange that he was reporting to a prison to begin his military duty. Most men reported to camps for training. He had no idea what was ahead for him at Urakami prison in Nagasaki.

He only knew he wanted to end the war as soon as possible so he could return to his family and Tori in Hiroshima.

Tori could not hide her sadness as she walked back into her house. Her three sisters were preparing to leave for school, but they gathered around her to hear the news that Mieko was leaving Hiroshima.

Her youngest sister, Machiko, only four years old, recalled something Mieko would do to make Tori smile. She went outside to their garden, picked three white roses, and ran back and placed them on Tori's lap. She also tried to give Tori one of the copper bracelets Mieko had made for her and her next older sister, Yoshiko. Tori gave her a big hug, and kindly refused the bracelet.

"Don't worry Tori, he'll come back," Machiko said.

They all knew how close Tori and Mieko had become. Yoshiko tried to lighten the mood.

"This war will soon be over and everyone will be coming home. We should look to the future and prepare for their return. Let's begin working on a play this week that will celebrate our country's victory." Yoshiko gave a nod to her other siblings. "Kazuko and Sachiko, you can work on the costumes and the boys will work on building a stage in the backyard." Her two brothers, Kiyoshi and Minoru, liked that idea. They didn't want to have to stay in the house with the girls. Yoshiko continued. "Tori, you have always been the actress in the family. You can write a play that we can perform for our conquering heroes, can't you?"

Tori recognized her sisters' efforts to make her feel better and smiled knowingly.

"Of course," Tori said. "I'm sure we can put together a wonderful performance for the neighborhood. Thank you for trying to make me feel better." Tori recalled one of the mornings at the harbor. "Mieko told me that my family should always be held closest to my heart. Someday he and I will marry and all of you will be there by my side." She briefly envisioned the ceremony. "I know it will take some time, but I'll be fine."

The sisters left for school. They returned that afternoon and began plans to surprise Tori with a special evening meal. Yoshiko ran to a local Hiroshima open market, only blocks away from their home, and spent some of the money she had been saving to purchase meat. This was a rare occurrence in their household since the war had forced everything to be rationed. She returned home and combined a few chicken parts, the only available meat she could find at the market, with a bowlful of rice and a handful of vegetables picked from their meager garden. The sisters worked together, cutting and preparing food. They wanted desperately to make their oldest sister happy. They all knew men from the neighborhood who had left their families and had not come home alive. They shared Tori's concern for Mieko.

Yoshiko asked her mother, Fumiko, to lure Tori out of the house while they prepared their surprise meal. She suggested a walk down by the harbor. Fumiko intercepted Tori on her return from school and they walked the mile and a half to the harbor. Tori took her mother to the refuge. It was the first time in years that Tori had been at the harbor without Mieko. Tori and Fumiko sat on the boulders and watched the sunset.

Tori looked at her mother and sobbed. They both knew how many boys had been killed in the war. Just the previous month Tori's two cousins died in a battle on an island in the Pacific.

Fumiko held Tori's hand in hers.

"You must have faith. The Emperor has powers that these Americans have not even seen yet. We will win this war and everything will be back to normal soon."

Tori shook her head and disagreed.

"No, mother, the Emperor does not have the answers. He only speaks of conquering our enemies, never of forgiving them. That is not the key to power."

They both sat quietly for a few moments listening to the gulls screeching and fighting for leftover remnants of fish near a returning fishing boat.

She squeezed her mother's hand.

"There is something else," Tori said. "I've never told anyone. Do you remember the day I fell into the ocean?"

"Why, yes dear," her mother said.

"That day God told me that Mieko would save me."

Fumiko nodded her head knowingly.

"Yes, dear, we remember you telling us that."

Tori hesitated and then said,

"Well, what I never told anyone is that God said Mieko would save me so that I could save him. What does that mean, mother? Was I supposed to keep him from going to war?"

Fumiko hugged Tori to her breast and calmly replied,

"I'm not sure, but I think that God must have meant that your love for Mieko would save him. Save him from becoming a demon like so many other men become during times of war. Maybe that's what he meant. Now let's go home. Your sisters have a surprise waiting for you."

They walked back home down the dirt trail and, together with her father, brothers, and sisters, spent the night eating and singing. They said prayers for their country and slept soundly, dreaming of peace.

Tori awakened early and made her way to the refuge down by the water's edge. There she stood and prayed for Mieko as the sun rose over Kusatsu Harbor.

Chapter 5

THE PRISON

Mieko was picked up at the Nagasaki bus station by an army staff car that deposited him inside the walls of Urakami Prison. His letter instructed him to report to Colonel Ho-kama. It was night when they arrived and the prison was quiet, save for an inmate who was playing a familiar Japanese folk song on his flute. Mieko was marched in to a small musty office in the corner of the compound. A desk with a typewriter sat in the middle of the room. A green file folder rested on the edge of the desk with Mieko's name written on the lower margin. On one wall hung a brown tattered map of the prison, showing details of the cellblocks. On the wall behind the desk hung a framed picture of a middle-aged woman in a green dress sitting at a table in a restaurant. Mieko stared at it for a moment. The colonel entered the office.

"That's my wife, Susheko," the colonel said. "I haven't seen her in two years. She writes almost every day wanting me to come home. Of course, I can't. Not until our work is done here."

"She's lovely," Mieko politely noted.

Colonel Hokama was a fifty-five-year-old stout man with thick glasses. His hair was thinning and was plastered to his head with gel. He looked worn. The colonel introduced himself.

"Before this war I managed the main research laboratory of the largest pharmaceutical company in Japan. Like you, I worked to save lives through medicine. Now life is different for all of us." In fact, Colonel Hokama was tired; tired of war and killing, the only thing he'd known for the past several years. The prison had become his laboratory and the laboratory his prison. The colonel looked at Mieko and, for a moment, envied his youth. "I've been in this prison for over two years, and I won't be leaving until we make the necessary discoveries. I hope you can help us. I want to see my wife again."

"I'll try my best, sir."

Colonel Hokama walked to the side of the desk in his stocking feet and picked up the folder with Mieko's name on it. His boots were sitting by the door, waiting to be polished by one of the prisoners. He examined his new recruit up and down, looked briefly through the folder, and in a quiet voice explained to Mieko why he had been brought to the prison.

"We have watched your progress for the past year. Your findings with regard to the infection research project were noteworthy. We think some of your research can now help our team of scientists to finalize our plans for ending this war within the next twelve months."

"What are your plans, sir?" Mieko asked.

"We have put together some of the greatest scientific minds in Japan here at Urakami Prison to discover a biological or chemical weapon that we can use to end this war. We have made many discoveries, but have yet to find the breakthrough we have sought." The colonel undid his waistcoat. "Your progress in treating infections may help us to make that breakthrough. You will assist Dr. Akiyama and run whatever tests he needs. Report to him in the morning. Good night."

Mieko was escorted out of the office and directed to his quarters. He opened the door to a tiny room near the solitary confinement cellblock. It looked like one of the cells he had passed in the cellblock corridor. It was painted a dark khaki green. The room had a small iron bed frame with a stained mattress, a sink with two rusted faucet handles, and a desk and chair sitting in the corner near the door. A pillow and folded woolen blanket lay at the foot of the bed.

Mieko was afraid and confused. His work had always centered on saving lives. Now he was being asked to create a doomsday virus. He knew this type of work was forbidden by all wartime conventions.

"Had the war really come to this?" He wondered, *"Were we, the supreme Japanese, really going to resort to using illegal weapons to win the war?"*

He knew he had no choice but to do as he was ordered or risk being imprisoned himself as a traitor. The next morning Mieko reported to Dr. Akiyama. As Mieko opened the door to the laboratory, Dr. Akiyama shouted,

"Sit down, shut up, and observe. I will speak to you after we finish here."

Mieko sat and watched as a Japanese prisoner was wrestled into the room and forced down into a chair. His arms and legs were strapped to the chair, immobilizing him completely. One of the doctors walked up to the side of the man and pulled out a syringe.

"No, no," the man screamed, "Don't kill me. I've done nothing wrong. Please, no, don't."[2]

"Start the timer." The doctor told his assistant.

The man's screaming intensified as the room full of researchers stood by and observed. The doctor stuck the needle in the man's arm and injected him with a red serum. His screaming stopped. His eyes

---

[2] Author's note: At this point my wife and I stopped the videotape and sent our three daughters to bed for the evening. Until this writing, we never shared the rest of Mieko's story with them.

showed a pain that Mieko would never forget. Within thirty seconds the man's mouth began foaming. He began to experience severe seizures from head to toe like nothing Mieko had ever witnessed.

At the fifteen-minute mark his eyes rolled up into his head, showing the whites of his eyes, and his convulsions began to lessen. He raised his head quickly and expelled a primal scream that Mieko would never forget. A few seconds later he was dead.

Mieko felt nauseous. The doctor spoke to the observers.

"This is unacceptable, far too slow." Dr. Akiyama was dismayed. He barked at his research team. "If we can't achieve death in five minutes or less we will never be able to use it. Go back and combine it with the formula we used yesterday. Let's test that one later today."

Mieko could hardly believe his ears.

"Another test later today?" he wondered. "Another man to die?"

Dr. Akiyama motioned for Mieko to follow him into another office. The doctor stood near the only window in the office. He was mean and hardened due to the work and the frustrations he faced every day. Although he was only thirty-six years old, the doctor had aged decades since he started working at the prison two years before. He was also impatient, and, more importantly, he had grown pessimistic about ever finding a way to win the war. He turned to look out the window. It faced an open field surrounded by barbed-wire fences.

"I do not have time for inefficiency. Our research has stalled recently and we need new ideas." Dr. Akiyama was visibly upset with the test results. "I know the work you've been doing and I believe you may bring some new thinking to our methods. That's why I requested you. Your current study regarding the infections our men have been contracting in China was brilliant."

Mieko put his hands in his pockets and looked down at the floor.

"Thank you, sir. We were starting to make some real progress over the past six months."

34

The doctor stopped and removed his glasses.

"Tomorrow you will begin research on the new plants and insects we've discovered in the past month in South Africa. Our agents continue to scour the world in hopes of finding new lethal organisms." Dr. Akiyama's eyes narrowed. "We need to find an organism that has the capability of infecting thousands of people. That is why you are here. The emperor needs us to find a weapon we can use to win this war. And we need it soon."

"I understand." Mieko felt the medallion against his chest and thought of Tori standing at the harbor.

Dr. Akiyama fingered some mail and looked sharply at Mieko.

"You're wondering about the prisoners, aren't you? The prison serves two purposes for us. We are safer here because the Americans do not see prisons as bombing targets. Most importantly, the prison provides us with live test specimens."

"But who are these prisoners?" Mieko asked.

"Most of the prisoners here at Urakami are of the worst kind: murderers, traitors, and other worthless scum. They are criminals of the state with no future. The emperor has given us permission to use all of them in our research." The doctor could tell Mieko was repulsed by the idea. "If it offends you, keep in mind that if we can develop a weapon to end the war sooner, their deaths could save thousands of our countrymen's lives." Dr. Akiyama handed a clipboard to Mieko. "Here, go observe for the rest of the day. Bring your notes back to me tonight. Tomorrow we'll set you up in your own laboratory and you can begin your own research protocol." He paused and stared squarely into Mieko's eyes. "Mieko, we need this weapon, and we need it soon."

At Dr. Akiyama's dismissal, Mieko left the office. As he walked down the dark hallway of the prison, the odors of the prisoners in the surrounding cells made him nauseous. He spotted a bucket and vomited into it. Even with all of the research he had done at the hospital, he had never seen a man die like that.

It was a sight he would become hardened to, for over the next several months Mieko's own tests would result in several hundred prisoners being killed. He felt part of his own spirit die with each prisoner's death.

Six months later in late July of 1945, Mieko and his team were in the final stages of testing a strain of virus in a new species of bees discovered in both the African and California deserts. The bees were new and un-named. They had small red stripes on their thoraxes and carried a virus that created the breakthrough the researchers were looking for.

This virus acted differently from anything they had ever developed before. When injected into the body, it attacked the whole immune system, rendering it useless to even the most minor infection. The results were devastating. They began to focus on how they could adapt the virus to be spread in other ways.

Dr. Akiyama was correct in thinking that Mieko would bring a different perspective to the testing. The bee virus was a breakthrough. However, Mieko and his team of researchers still needed to devise a way to implement the virus into an explosive device. Mieko believed it would only be a matter of months before they could find the solution and win the war.

Mieko was motivated to find the solution. He wanted to see Tori again. Months had passed since he'd last seen her and he knew that the sooner the war ended, the sooner he could get home.

Because of the secret nature of their work, the workers at the prison had been forbidden to correspond with anyone outside the prison walls. Mieko yearned to tell Tori that his team had discovered a possible solution that would end the war. His chance to tell her would come much sooner than he had imagined.

Chapter 6

On the morning of August 6, 1945, Tori took her usual early walk down to the boulders at the harbor to pray. The refuge was only a mile and a half from the center of Hiroshima, but her view of the city was completely blocked by large boulders that had been piled one on top of the other to fight erosion at the harbor. The light morning haze lifted to expose many boats in the harbor. Tori sat down to begin her prayers. She heard the drone of an engine in the sky above.

Suddenly, a tremendous flash lit up the sky. The boulders shielded Tori from the initial blast, but the aftershock caused her to lose her balance and fall into the harbor waters. The harbor waters saved her from the waves of fire and heat that swept the city following the blast. She stayed in the water, protected from the inferno she watched erupt around her. Hours later, when she finally pulled herself from the water and looked over the boulders toward the city, all she could see were flames. Flames engulfed everything in sight that hadn't been flattened by the blast. The water she had come out of was filled with bodies, swollen and burned, some still alive crying out in agony.

The first atomic bomb had been dropped on Hiroshima. Within a span of seconds, thousands of people vanished from the face of the earth. Thousands more were left homeless and exposed to radiation that would haunt them and their children for decades to follow.

Even though Tori was only a mile-and-a-half away at the harbor, she found it almost impossible to travel the streets. Fires broke out everywhere. Not until the afternoon was Tori finally able to find her way back to where her home had stood earlier that morning. On her way she saw what appeared to be shadows of people burned into the concrete walks. But they were not shadows, they were markings left on the concrete as a result of bodies that vaporized instantly. Tori's neighborhood had been close to the epicenter of the explosion. Almost everything and everyone had been reduced to ash. Noticeably most color had disappeared, replaced by hues of brown, gray, and black. There were no trees, no buildings, and no vehicles.

There also was no sign of her family. Her house and everything in it were destroyed, leaving hardly a hint that anything had existed there only hours earlier. She knew her sisters and parents were dead. Mieko's family was also gone. The entire neighborhood was destroyed. Most of the city had been leveled or was burning. Dozens of people were wandering the area. Tori did not recognize anyone. She was alone and afraid.

As she looked through the rubble where her home used to stand, she spotted a pile of ashes with what was left of two copper bracelets. They had melted together, as if her sisters were now locked in an eternal embrace. Her family was gone. Now only Mieko remained.

Some people were screaming, but many others wandered in silence. People bearing burns and injuries never before imaginable walked the streets looking for help. But there was no help for the victims.

Tori saw a woman sitting by a shattered block of concrete that was formerly a pillar at the base of a Hindu temple. The woman was naked and burned from the waist up, staring into space through burned and

38

swollen eyes that were surrendering to her pain. Her shirt, burned into her back, left a windowpane pattern in her roasted skin. Her burned arm had burst open exposing bone.

An old man, blinded by flying glass in the blast, begged for help. A large patch of his hair was burned off his scalp, and blood was pouring from two wounds near his neck.

Tori spotted a young girl crawling around some rubble, looking for her family. When the girl turned to face her, Tori saw her right arm had been severed at the elbow, probably from flying glass or debris. She held the stump in her left hand, wrapped only in a blood-soaked kerchief. Burns stretched across the girl's naked torso from her shoulders to her knees. Her clothes had been blown off in the blast, and her skin was hanging from her arms and hand as if peeled from a piece of burned fruit.

Tori disappeared into a shell of shock and fear. She began wandering away from the city until she was on the outskirts. She recovered enough to realize she needed to escape from this horror. Her only hope for her own survival was to find Mieko. He would know what to do. She began walking in a shock-induced trance to the only place she could think of, Urakami prison in Nagasaki. She only had the clothes on her back as she began her journey to the prison that was about two-hundred miles south of Hiroshima.

Night fell, but she kept walking. She was far out of the city by nightfall, back into areas that were more recognizable, areas that still had homes, plants, and people. She was determined to find Mieko. He was all she had left in the world. Around midnight of the first day, a man driving to the south stopped and asked if he could help her. She rode with him through the night, sleeping briefly, periodically waking to nightmares of what had happened that morning. Shortly after daybreak, the driver dropped her off near a small general store. They had covered over one-hundred miles overnight. She was halfway to Mieko.

She walked inside the store and looked around. The storekeeper and his wife were beginning to clean the floor. Tori was hungry and saw an opportunity. She spoke to them.

"I'd be happy to clean your floor if you could spare me some food. I haven't eaten since leaving Hiroshima last night."

The couple were taken aback and took a break from their cleaning while they listened to Tori tell them what happened at Hiroshima the day before.

The shopkeeper gave her some hope.

"I'm driving about twenty miles south later today to the fish market. I can give you a ride. Maybe we can find someone else at the market who can help you from there."

Tori thanked him.

The wife gave her some food and led her to the back of the store where she was able to rest.

Later that afternoon when they arrived at the fish market, the shopkeeper was able to arrange another ride for her with one of the fishmongers who had come to the market from a town farther south, just forty miles north of Nagasaki. She rode with the fishmonger for a few hours, retelling her story once again. When the fishmonger dropped her by the side of the road that evening of August 7th, he gave her a heavy woolen blanket for comfort and some additional pieces of fish, rice balls, and water.

She slept in a field that night and on the morning of August 8th began the walk to Urakami Prison. She did not see a vehicle the entire day, but was able to walk over thirty miles before she had to stop and sleep on a soft grassy mound near the roadside. She was only ten miles from the prison. Exhausted from her journey, she pulled the borrowed blanket around her body like a cocoon. She lay down and disappeared into the deepest sleep she ever experienced.

She dreamed that Mieko was talking to her. She could feel his hand on her shoulder. She tried to tell him about their families and the bombing, but when she opened her mouth to speak, nothing would come out. She thought she heard him whisper.

"God Bless you, I must go and find my family in Hiroshima."

She again tried to tell him they were all dead, but no sound would come out of her mouth. She remained asleep until morning.

Chapter 7

On the evening of August 7, the news of Hiroshima's disaster made it to Urakami prison. Mieko was in his laboratory with his team finishing a series of tests when one of his researchers threw the door open and announced that the Americans dropped an atomic bomb on Hiroshima. Mieko's face went ashen. He had read of the possibilities of such a bomb and was aware of some of the work being done by his own country to create one.

Within minutes, Colonel Hokama came through the door and tried to settle everyone in the laboratory.

"Listen up, men. I know all types of rumors are circulating that an enormous bomb devastated Hiroshima. We have reliable information that says it was a large squadron of bombers, not a single bomb. Stay focused on your work, men, we need results now more than ever."

Mieko immediately ran to Colonel Hokama to request a leave. He wanted to go home immediately to Hiroshima to see if his family needed help. Colonel Hokama denied his request.

"Mieko, you need to understand. None of us can leave until we finalize the weapons project we've been working on." Colonel Hokama tried to reason with Mieko. He needed to keep his scientists working. "I can't let anyone leave the prison until we have finished. I'm sorry. However, I can tell you that our contacts in Hiroshima tell us that, although there was a lot of damage, there seems to be only minor casualties."

Mieko could sense the colonel was lying. He understood why.

More reports came in later that night. There had been massive destruction in Hiroshima. Thousands of people had perished. Mieko knew the importance of his project, but remembered what his grandfather had told him.

"Live your life for your family and you will live happily."

Mieko decided to plan an escape. During the next day he conspired with one of his fellow researchers, Dr. Yoshitaka Tamura. They devised an escape plan for that night. He could depend on Yoshitaka. They had become close friends in the short time they had been at the prison together. Like Mieko, Yoshitaka had been a child prodigy, and the two of them had connected on many levels.

Together they worked out the details of the escape. Every night a truck came and hauled away the dead prisoners who were test victims that day. Mieko, along with Yoshitaka, enlisted the aid of the truck driver. Yoshitaka wrapped Mieko into a body sack and stacked him in the truck on top of the dead prisoners. About five miles from the prison the driver stopped to unload the bodies for burning. He helped Mieko out of the burial sack. Mieko had escaped from Urakami prison, bound to find his family in Hiroshima. From that point he would be on his own to find his way back to Hiroshima.

Mieko had not traveled far when he happened across what appeared to be a beggar by the side of the road. He could tell from her hair adornments that it was a woman. He was about to ask her if she'd like some food, when he realized that she was sleeping soundly under a heavy blanket, her face partially covered by her hair. He put his hand on her shoulder, but she would not wake up. Mieko thought she must be a homeless victim of the war.

He whispered.

"God Bless you, I must go and find my family in Hiroshima."

He left her sleeping and continued on his journey.

Tori awoke early just before sunrise on the morning of August 9th. She remembered her dream of Mieko and could not shake the feeling that he had been right there talking to her.

As she stood to finish her journey to the prison, a passing truck stopped and offered her a ride. The driver took her all the way to the gates of Urakami prison. When she arrived, she asked to see Mieko. Colonel Hokama was told of her request and had her delivered to his office.

As she walked through the dark prison to the colonel's office, prisoners whistled and howled at seeing a woman in their midst for the first time in months. She saw a guard hit one of the whistling prisoners in the face with a club, drawing blood from his nose. She heard a blood-curdling scream from behind one of the doors they passed.

She entered Colonel Hokama's office.

"I understand that you wish to see one of our doctors. May I ask why?" He inquired.

"Sir, my name is Tori Yamaki. I've traveled for two days from Hiroshima to tell Mieko that his family has all died." Tori continued. "The explosion and fires killed all of them. I am the only person left alive from both of our families."

"So, you are Tori," the colonel said. "Mieko has mentioned you many times. You are every bit as pretty as he said."

She caught a glimpse through the doorway of a prisoner in chains being led to the laboratory.

"Sir, we are going to marry after the war. I didn't know what else to do but come and find him. He is all I have left and I am all that he has left. May I please see him, sir?"

"Yes, of course. Please have a seat," Colonel Hokama replied, notifying an aide to find Mieko. "While we find him, would you please tell me more about the bombing?"

"Yes, sir, I'll try." Tori answered, taking a seat next to the colonel's desk. "I was standing at the harbor when it hit."

"It? You mean the squadron of bombers?" the colonel asked.

"No sir, I never even saw any planes. It was just one massive explosion. The fires were everywhere. And afterwards it rained a black rain, a horrible black rain." Tori felt tears come into her eyes. "Colonel, my grandfather used to tell me stories about wars, but he never described anything so horrible. I saw ghosts of people burned into walls and sidewalks. The entire city was in flames. I pray no one ever again has to see such devastation."

"One explosion? Are you sure?" The colonel asked.

"Yes, sir, I am positive. There was only one explosion. But it was so powerful . . . the entire city . . . people burning . . . children crying." Tori buried her face in her hands and began to cry as she remembered the horrid details.

"One explosion put an entire city into flame?" The colonel made his way over to a chair and sat down.

He thought for a moment about what he knew of the atomic bomb research being done by his own country. He knew if the Americans had developed it first, Japan would certainly lose the war and his own research would never be needed. If her story of this bomb was true, his fight was ending. No one could defend against more attacks like this. Life in Japan would be changing sooner than anyone had expected. As he looked at Tori, he realized that she epitomized his country's plight. She'd lost almost everything and was looking for the last ray of hope that existed for her. He wanted to help her. His own mission had become meaningless.

The aide returned and whispered in the colonel's ear.

The colonel looked shocked but spoke to Tori.

"Mieko is missing. We haven't been able to locate him. We think he left the prison last night without permission. He requested a leave yesterday to go back to Hiroshima to find you and his family, but I denied it." The colonel knew that Mieko's absence no longer was a concern if the story of this bomb was true. The colonel wanted to help Tori. "I am sure that Hiroshima is his destination. I can have a driver take you to the edge of town, but I'm afraid you'll have to find your way back to Hiroshima on your own." The colonel looked at his aide, thought for a second, and continued. "Also, I have to let you know that I will be sending some military police to retrieve Mieko and bring him back to Urakami. After hearing your description of the damage in Hiroshima, we need his help now more than ever." Colonel Hokama said this only to maintain a front in the presence of his subordinates. He was already feeling his own sense of hopelessness. "Tori, you look exhausted. Please rest here for a few hours. I'll have some food brought up for you." Colonel Hokama then made arrangements for a driver to take her to the edge of town later that morning.

"Thank you, sir," she said. "I will find him. I must find him."

The colonel wished her luck and decided he would not send anyone to find Mieko until the following day.

Later that morning, after Tori had rested and eaten, the colonel's driver dropped her at the edge of town and returned to the prison.

She looked back down the hill at the prison in the distance. She thought of Mieko. She thought about how he escaped to find her and his family. Tori became excited with the prospects of meeting up with him in Hiroshima. It would not be hard to find him since there were few places left to go for shelter. She sat for ten minutes and then stood up to begin her long journey back to Hiroshima. It was almost midday as she looked back toward the prison for the last time. She heard another engine high up in the sky. It paralyzed her.

47

Time stood still as her thoughts flashed back to Kusatsu Harbor only days before. She could feel it happening again. Another flash lit up the sky. She was blown to the ground.

The second atomic bomb annihilated Nagasaki.

Urakami prison was only yards from the epicenter and, in a few split seconds, was reduced to ashes. Colonel Hokama, Dr. Akiyama, and all of the soldiers and prisoners died instantly. No one would be sent to retrieve Mieko.

Mieko was the lone survivor of the Urakami Prison weapons research project. He alone knew secrets no one else would ever discover.

The rest of the city was demolished instantly and fires covered the city. Tens of thousands were killed in an explosion that was hundreds of times more powerful than the bomb that had exploded on Hiroshima days earlier.

As for Tori, this time she was not shielded from the blast by boulders or water, but she was quite a ways from the epicenter. She sustained severe flash burns over much of her face and body. The blast knocked her unconscious, and she fell face down in the road.

She lay there for several hours before an old woman discovered her. The woman took Tori to a makeshift hospital set up near the outskirts of town. Tori had become one of a handful of people who survived both atomic bomb explosions.

But survival carried a large price. When she finally regained consciousness days later in the hospital, she found that her world had changed radically. Japan's war was over, but Tori's battles were just beginning. Bandages covered over half of her body, including most of her head. Her clothing had been blown off leaving massive burns on her torso and legs.

She was transferred with many of the other survivors to a hospital in a nearby town and for two months Tori was forced to stay in bed. Her burns were rubbed with oil three times daily, and her leg wrappings were changed every morning. The pain was unbearable, but she continued to pray and thank God for sparing her life and for helping Mieko to escape the night before the blast. She began to walk in the third month, weeks before the doctors predicted. She constantly surprised the doctors with every aspect of her recovery.

It wasn't until that third month that Tori saw the full impact of the situation. When her bandages were removed from her head she was able, for the first time since the bombing, to see her reflection in a mirror.

She did not recognize the thing staring back at her. It was monstrous. Her skin had melted to partially cover her left eye. Her left ear was a now a small flap of skin, and her hair was burned off half of her scalp. As she stared into the mirror, she felt that she was looking at some creature from another world.

Her first thoughts were of Mieko. She longed to see him, but he would never recognize her. Worse yet, her beauty that he had always loved had disappeared and had been replaced by something hideous. She could never face him. Yet, in her heart, she knew finding Mieko was the only hope she had for living. She yearned to find him and just be near him. That was all she wanted.

Over the next few months Tori recovered and helped others do the same. She thought about what she must do. She could never expect Mieko to love her now, but she could still love him. She had no one else in the world. She needed to find him and be near him without revealing her true identity. She never wanted to let him know what had happened. Tori could not bear the thought of Mieko pitying her instead of loving her.

She yearned to be near Mieko. Somehow, some way, she had to find a way to be near him. Otherwise, she could find no reason for living.

Chapter 8

On August 11th, Mieko reached the city of Hiroshima. His journey had lasted three days. He heard many stories about the destruction from refugees fleeing in the opposite direction. On the last day, along the roads leading into town, he witnessed hundreds of refugees in makeshift tents, begging for food, looking for water. He saw others wandering with burn injuries all over their bodies that seethed with maggots and white ooze.

The stories of the disaster did not prepare him for what he saw as he entered the outskirts of the city that day. The entire city was flattened, reduced to ashes. The odor of burning flesh penetrated his nostrils, and he saw children wandering aimlessly. There were no hospitals, no schools, and no temples. Thousands of buildings had been demolished. It took him hours to discern where his neighborhood had once stood.

When he arrived at the place where his home previously stood, he saw a lifeless pile of rubble. Fire had swept over most of the area charring everything in sight. No one could have survived. Mieko suddenly realized that his family, the family his grandfather had told him to protect, was gone. He realized Tori and her family must have perished as well. He sat down in the rubble and sank into a deep depression.

He was totally alone. He contemplated suicide. He fell asleep weeping for his family and Tori.

When he awoke the next morning he went straight to one of the volunteer centers and began to help with the cleanup taking place throughout Hiroshima. As he walked the city, he saw firsthand how brutal the war had been to his people. He saw hundreds of orphaned children who had been exposed to the blast wandering and rummaging through trash piles. There were not enough doctors available to give them medical attention. In the week following August 6th, people who had survived the blast began to get sick. Many became nauseous, unable to hold food down. Others began losing their hair. The sick people kept getting sicker and dying with each new day.

On August 14th, after a day of volunteering at one of the makeshift treatment centers on the outskirts of the town, Mieko was confronted by a young boy and his sister, asking him for money. They had both lost their hair and were suffering from burns covering their bodies. No one had stepped forward to help them. It dawned on Mieko that this could have been his family begging for mercy. His feelings of hopelessness began to turn into anger. He helped them get settled at one of the centers, but he could not control his growing anger.

Mieko thought about the prison and his research. In all the time they were researching weapons, neither Colonel Hokama nor Dr. Akiyama ever discussed killing civilians to win the war. Mieko did not believe Japan would ever have resorted to mass killing of civilians, certainly not like this. It was horrific, this instant slaughter of innocent people. His anger gave him energy and life. Mieko wanted revenge.

On the afternoon of August 15th he decided that he wanted to get back to Urakami Prison and finish the work he had started. He saw an army truck stopped near his hut, dropping off supplies for the first aid shelter. Mieko approached the driver.

"I'm with the army and I need to get back to my station. Can you at least help me get out of this city?"

"Where are you heading?" The driver asked.

"To a prison in Nagasaki. I am working on a weapon that will put an end to this war." Mieko replied

"Nagasaki?" The driver exclaimed, "They bombed it the same as Hiroshima days ago. Haven't you heard?"

Mieko's volunteer efforts had secluded him from everything. He was completely unaware of the bombing in Nagasaki.

The driver reached over and turned on the truck radio. Reports of Japan's surrender blasted out of the speakers. That day, for the first time ever, the Japanese people heard Emperor Hirohito's voice as he surrendered.

The driver shouted at Mieko.

"The Emperor surrendered today. They say over a quarter of a million people have been killed by the bombs. The war is over. Go home."

Mieko's knees buckled beneath him. He looked at the driver.

"A quarter of a million people? No war to fight?" Mieko became angry. "How can there not be a war to fight? My family was all killed. They are all dead. Tori is dead." Mieko's rage showed as he yelled at the driver. "Japan must extract some kind of revenge for all of this death and destruction. Someone has to pay. I will not stop fighting this war." The driver became frightened as Mieko's yelling continued. "I will fight this war until we win."

On that day, August 15th, 1945, Mieko decided he would continue the fight against the Americans and seek revenge for his family's deaths. He felt that his country had no right to stop the war before his family and many others were avenged. If he had to continue alone, or with some of his co-workers from the prison, he would continue his work.

The driver of the truck reluctantly gave Mieko a ride to the closest army command post. It was there that Mieko learned that Urakami

Prison was completely destroyed. There was now no reason for him to return to Nagasaki. His life now focused solely on one destination. It was the only place where he could finish his war. He needed to find a way to get to the United States.

Mieko suddenly realized that he alone held the secret of the deadly virus. He only had to find a way to dispense it. He resolved to kill at least one American for every death the bombs in Hiroshima and Nagasaki had caused. The only number he had heard was a quarter of a million people. He did not know how he could do it, but he vowed to find a way.

Mieko secured a job at a local hospital and helped to treat the many burn victims while he saved his money for a trip to America.

Seven months after the bombings, in March of 1946, after Japan's formal surrender had taken place, he decided he would walk back down to Kusatsu Harbor and find passage to the United States. He recalled hearing Tori's aunt speak of the Japanese neighborhoods in San Francisco. He could fit in there and finish the work he had started at Urakami Prison. When he got to the harbor he saw the old harbormaster he met years ago on one of his morning walks with Tori. The man did not remember Mieko, but laughed when he asked for passage to America.

"America?" He asked, "Haven't you heard? They don't want more Japanese. They hate us. Why would you want to go where you're not welcome?"

"That's my concern, old man. Is there no way to get to America?" Mieko asked.

"Do you have any money?"

"A little." Mieko showed the man his savings. "But I am willing to work to pay my way. Just get me to America," Mieko said.

The harbormaster caught sight of the medallion hanging from Mieko's neck.

"What is that?"

Mieko pulled out the medallion Tori had given him.

"It is a great samurai's medal."

Mieko suddenly noticed that the medallion somehow looked different to him.

"Let me see it," the Harbormaster reached for the medallion. He carefully looked it over. Something about it caught his eye. He looked up at Mieko. "I will give you passage for the medallion, but you must work on the boat if you wish to eat."

Mieko considered the offer. The medallion was his last link to Tori. However, the medallion was no longer a source of inspiration. Instead, it had become a burden, a reminder of a love he would never have. The medallion would prove useful now. It would help him get to America to avenge her death. It seemed the right thing to do. He gave the medallion to the harbormaster.

Three days later, after months of waiting, Mieko's boat pulled out of Kusatsu Harbor on the south side of Hiroshima on a course for San Francisco. It was March 15th, 1946. The boat was about a quarter mile from shore when it passed the boulders where he and Tori had walked and talked of marriage.

When he looked toward the boulders he saw a figure standing in their old refuge. He imagined the figure to be Tori, standing by the rocks and praying. Mieko bowed his head and prayed for revenge.

After Tori regained her strength, she decided to work in the same hospital where she recovered from her injuries. She was put to work helping with the many young children orphaned by the bombings. Most of her days were spent oiling burns that covered the children's bodies. She would wrap arms and legs in gauze, being careful not to remove any more skin than had already fallen from them. She would talk to the children while she worked on them. She found that their wounds were far deeper than the burns on their skin.

One young girl, aged six, named Misako, reminded Tori of her own sister, Machiko. Misako's entire family died in the blast. Tori would arrive every morning to tend to Misako's burns. She would gently unwrap the bindings from her legs and carefully apply oils to Misako's burns. Tori would make Misako laugh with her funny stories about her own brothers and all of their mischief. Tori would bring her fruit and snacks or make her cranes from paper to hang near her mat. One day Misako gently put her hand on Tori's misshapen face.

"Tori, do I look like you? Is my face ugly, too?"

Tori laughed at her innocence.

"No, Misako, you are beautiful on the outside and the inside."

Misako smiled. "Thank you for being my friend, Tori."

Misako's burns were severe across her torso, legs, and back. Her hair began to fall out in December, and on February 20th of 1946, Tori made her final visit to Misako and held her hand as she passed away, dying of complications arising from pneumonia. Tori sank into a depression for the next few weeks, feeling like she had lost another sister.

She continued to work with many other patients and listened to many gruesome stories of burned family members who lived in pain, waiting to eventually die, knowing their fate, and understanding the futility of the doctors' efforts. Tori became grateful that her family died quickly and were spared similar agonies. She prayed for guidance in keeping these young victims hopeful for the future. She fought daily to keep other children from giving up on their lives. Tori knew that they were the generation who would have to rebuild the country.

But Misako's death hit Tori hard. She knew her work was important, but now she wanted to find Mieko. Seven months after the blast, in early March of 1946, Tori decided to travel back to Hiroshima. She knew Mieko must be there.

With the aid of a letter from her employer, she arrived in Hiroshima and promptly got a job at a temporary hospital that was located close to where she used to live, only a short walk away from Kusatsu Harbor. She took up residence in a makeshift dormitory. The facility was made up of sixteen large rooms. Each room had ten cots and shared an outdoor shower and toilet with all of the other residents.

On her second day she met two women who had lost their families in the blast. Kazuko, 43, had lost her husband and three sons. She had been in Kyoto visiting her cousin on the day of the blast. Masumi had just celebrated her 27th birthday a few days before Tori arrived in Hiroshima. She lost her husband and two small daughters in the blast. She, too, had been out of town, picking up some supplies for her husband's business when the bomb exploded.

58

Kazuko and Masumi took Tori under their wings and helped her get settled at the hospital.

Tori told Masumi and Kazuko about Mieko and asked if they knew of anyone who fit his description. Masumi thought she had met Mieko, but couldn't remember where. Tori continued to ask other workers. Some people told her they previously worked with a man who fit the description she gave, but no one knew his whereabouts. She became hopeful. She knew he was alive and in Hiroshima. It would just be a matter of time before she found him.

Tori's burns continued to heal but now were developing into scars, some large and unsightly, called keloid scars. The keloid scars were burned areas that became hardened and were almost impossible to remove. Most of her keloids were on her back. They had not shown up on her face. Her pain was constant, but mild. Her prayers continued to give her comfort.

On Tori's fourth night back in Hiroshima, as they were walking to the dormitory, Masumi asked Tori what she prayed for. Tori's eyes lit up. She rarely got to share her beliefs and she knew both Masumi and Kazuko harbored great hatred for the Americans for what they had done to their families.

"I pray that no other countries will ever use such powers in war. I pray for the strength to forgive the Americans. I know that it was their leaders who made the decision to drop the bombs, not the civilians. I pray to forgive them because forgiveness from us is imperative in order for everyone to live peacefully."

Masumi and Kazuko listened. Over time they would understand. Tori had that power over others, power that gave people hope in hopeless situations.

But Masumi and Kazuko could not protect Tori from the rest of her own people. Tori was now a victim of the atomic blasts who became known as the hibakusha. Employers would not hire them. Even patients coming to the hospital with ordinary illnesses would keep away from the obvious blast victims, the hibakusha. The public came to realize that the hibakusha's health problems were completely unpredictable. People did not know if the problems were contagious in some way. Fear and ignorance led everyone to shun them. Tori maintained a low-key existence at the hospital. Masumi and Kazuko shielded Tori as much as possible from the everyday prejudice that surrounded them.

A week after she arrived in Hiroshima, on March 15th, she walked down to their old refuge by the harbor. It felt good to return to the one place that brought back the strongest memories of Mieko.

A boat horn in the distance caught her attention. She looked up to see a large ship with a British insignia on the side heading out to sea. She remembered talking to Mieko about boarding a ship some day to explore the world after they were married. She bowed her head and said a prayer of forgiveness and thanks. She knew God was leading her to Mieko.

Chapter   10

Nine years passed as Tori searched in vain for Mieko. She was twenty-eight years old. She would walk to the harbor each morning to pray and then go to the hospital and work for twelve-to-sixteen hours. At night, with Masumi or Kazuko by her side, Tori combed the streets of Hiroshima, asking everyone she met if they had seen Mieko. All of her pictures of Mieko were destroyed in the bombing, so she could only provide verbal descriptions to those she met. His trail had vanished. She had no way of knowing that Mieko had been on that boat headed for San Francisco on that March day in 1946.

By 1955, Tori had become a popular figure in the hospital. Despite her own disfigurement, she managed to bring optimism and hope for the future to many disconsolate patients. She focused her energies to help place some of the orphaned children in private homes and made it her routine to visit them periodically to check their progress.

Burn patients sought her out in an effort to find peace in their disjointed existence. She spent time with other hibakusha, who had become ostracized because of their exposure to the atomic bomb. Slowly she began to see that her life was taking a new direction. She thought her distorted features would lead to a life of loneliness. Instead, she was finding that many people sought her presence and were inspired by her will to live and carry on with her life.

Most of all, she found that other victims admired her ability to forgive the Americans for what they had done to her and her family. Her belief that forgiveness was the only path to the future was the greatest single source of inspiration for many other patients. The doctors all agreed that her positive influence undoubtedly helped save many patients' lives by instilling them with a stronger will to live.

It was because of these qualities that one of the hospital administrators, Dr. Ishihara, pulled her aside one day.

"Tori, we have some good news. We've been asked by the government to find a group of women who have severe burn injuries like yours to go to the United States for a chance to heal their wounds."

Dr. Ishihara laid down the files he was holding.

"The Americans have volunteered their hospitals and expert surgeons in an effort to help repair some of the damage that the bombs created. The Americans have surgical techniques called plastic surgery that are more advanced than we have here in Japan. We'd like you to be part of this group of women." Dr. Ishihara was surprised when he saw that Tori was not immediately enthused over this opportunity. "This may be the only chance you will ever have to repair your burns. They claim to be able to shape skin and get rid of scar tissue so that you would never know it existed. We have seen pictures of their patients and, quite frankly, it is almost miraculous. The group will be leaving next week." Dr. Ishihara continued, "Tori, with all of the wonderful work you've done here at the hospital, we all agreed that you should be given the first opportunity."

Tori thought for a few minutes. She looked at Dr. Ishihara and smiled.

"Thank you, but if I were to change how I look now, how would I ever communicate with these people in the hospital who need me so much? How could I face them with no scars? Most of them will never get a chance to be healed." Tori pointed to her scars. "They rely on me for strength. They see what I have gone through and it gives them hope that they can persevere. No, I'm afraid not. Please send someone else."

"Are you sure?" Dr. Ishahara pleaded. "Everyone here would like to see you go."

"No," Tori replied, "I must stay here. Besides, you know, I still must find Mieko. I know he is here somewhere in the city."

After nine years of searching, Tori's hope of finding Mieko had become more of a delusional obsession. Masumi and Kazuko continued to feed her delusion with weekly excursions into the city to find Mieko, believing it was the one hope in her life that made her truly happy.

"I understand." Dr. Ishihara was disappointed, but saw more clearly why this woman was so respected. With that, Tori walked back to her dormitory.

The next morning Tori took her usual walk down to the harbor. After her morning prayers she started her walk back to the hospital when a young boy stopped her. He couldn't have been more than thirteen years old. His clothes were dirty and torn. He had a burn scar across his brow.

"Do you know if there are any jobs down here at the harbor?" he asked. "I told my mother that I would get some money for food for my family. They're counting on me. My father was killed in the war and our home was destroyed in the bombing. I am the man of the family now."

"No, I don't know of any work." Tori said. "But if you follow me, maybe we can find someone who does."

His looks reminded her of Mieko when he was thirteen. She led him to the harbormaster's shack and asked if there was work available for a strong young boy. The man rose slowly from his seat in the shack. When he first saw Tori, he was so startled by her face that he could not answer. He tried to keep from staring and quickly became embarrassed.

He finally looked at the boy.

"Work? Here? Why, yes, I think we may have a few jobs that need done. Can you come back in the morning? I will find some work for you."

"Yes, thank you, thank you, sir. I'll be here at sunrise," the boy said.

Before he could take off running for home to tell his mother the news, Tori pulled a few coins from her pocket. One of the coins accidentally fell to the ground. She handed the remaining coins to the boy and told him to buy some rice for his family for dinner. The harbormaster bent over to pick up the coin she dropped. As he bent over, the medallion Mieko had given him years ago came out from beneath his shirt. Tori caught sight of the medallion.

"Where did you get that?" she half screamed at the startled man.

"It was given to me many years ago by a man who was looking for passage to America."

"America?" Tori was shaking.

She told the harbormaster her story and offered to buy back the medallion, but he would not hear of it. Her story touched his soul. The harbormaster removed the medallion from his neck and gave it to Tori.

"When Mieko gave me this medallion, he told me it was special. This man looking at the sunrise must have been a powerful warrior. It has given me much inspiration and luck. Take it now and find your Mieko."

Tori knew what she must do. She immediately went to the hospital and contacted Dr. Ishihara.

"I have changed my mind. I want to go to America," she told him.

She explained what happened with the harbormaster and told him she did not care about the surgery, but that she wanted to go to America to find Mieko.

The doctor was pleased, but had to confront her.

"Tori, I can't send you with the other women unless you agree to have surgery. It will be in your best interest." He was adamant on that point. "Tori, this group of women . . . they are important. They represent healing between our two countries. The newspapers have already begun to write stories about the importance of the trip."

Tori thought for a moment. She did not want her name to be used.

"Doctor, I'll agree to have surgery if I can just get to America. Could I use a different name while I'm traveling? I don't want Mieko to find out I'm alive."

Dr. Ishihara saw no reason to deny her wish. He understood why she didn't want Mieko to know she was alive. He helped to make the special arrangements with the committee.

Dr. Ishihara was happy to hear that she had changed her mind. He knew the possibility of her finding Mieko was slim. He also knew her surgeries would be long and painful given the amount of scarring she had endured. He feared they might not be successful because of the severity of her burns. Although he had seen the pictures of the miracle surgery, he knew that this trip was more of a political gesture to ease the tensions between the United Stated and Japan.

Nevertheless, he was glad she was going. He could not offer her any type of hope through his hospital. This represented her only chance to regain just a little of her former beauty.

Tori bid farewell to Masumi and Kazuko and left the following Friday on a trip to America with a group of women who would become known to the world as "The Hiroshima Maidens."

Chapter 11

In March of 1946, when Mieko sailed from Kusatsu Harbor, he did not know that the crew was made up of Brits and Aussies. He was the only Japanese on board. One look at Mieko and tempers flared. The first night on the ship two of the British soldiers cornered him. One grabbed hold of him from behind while the other kicked him in the midsection and then hit him in the jaw.

"Damn Nip. Your people killed my brother. We oughta throw you overboard. They shoulda nuked the rest of your country." Mieko pretended that he did not speak English, a language he and Tori had learned together from her aunt. The Englishman continued. "My buddy was in one of your death marches. Were you there at Bataan? Maybe you led it." He struck another blow to Mieko's chest.

For three weeks Mieko endured beating after beating at the hands of the crewmen who used him as their target for the hatred they had built up for the Japanese during the war. Mieko did not fight back. Sometimes he laughed as they beat him. That made them angrier. At times they thought he was crazy. Other times he wished they would kill him. One night, a week before making port, the captain finally intervened.

"Men, the war is over. We've all lost family." He pointed at Mieko. "For all you know, this guy might have lost some family, too. Leave him be now. We all need to move on. Anyone touches him again and I'll personally throw you off this boat. Got it?"

The men grumbled, but no one laid a hand on Mieko after that.

In late April of 1946 Mieko landed in San Francisco, and, through the newspapers, found a Japanese family who had a room available to rent in the upstairs of their home.

He went there and was greeted at the door by Mrs. Mokado. She was a petite woman with a big smile. She invited him in and offered him tea while they waited for Mr. Mokado to finish washing up from his day at work.

Mr. Mokado entered the room. He noticed Mieko's unkempt appearance, the rips in his shirt and the mud on his shoes. He looked Mieko in the eye for almost a full minute. Mieko grew nervous. Mr. Mokado began to speak.

"My father came from Kyoto to San Francisco in 1924 and opened a fish market. He worked day and night to achieve the American Dream." Mieko did not understand why Mr. Mokado was telling him this. "Then, during World War II, the American Army gathered all of us and threw us into internment camps. Have you heard of those, son?"

"No, sir." Mieko had not heard anything of these camps.

Mr. Mokado continued. "The camps were built to prevent any of us from assisting the Japanese. But most of us considered ourselves to be Americans. Many people died in the camps, never seeing their American homes again. My father was one of those who died. Even with that, our family was one of the lucky ones." Mr. Mokado continued. "Before we were taken to the camp, our neighbor, Mr. Davis Blackshere, helped us. He was a good man."

Mr. Mokado stepped closer to Mieko. "Mr. Blackshere bought our store and then sold it back to me when we returned from the camps.

He refused to take any profit and he let me pay for it over time. It was the only way we were able to keep our shop."

Mr. Mokado sat down in the chair next to Mieko. He noticed the bruises on Mieko's arms from the beatings on the boat.

"I tell you this because I see something in your eyes that bothers me. Before you settle on living here, you need to know that many of these Americans are good people."

"I understand, sir," Mieko politely replied. He liked Mr. Mokado. He reminded him of his grandfather. Mieko then asked about the room. Mr. Mokado showed Mieko the small room in the upstairs of the house. Mieko asked what it would cost.

Mr. Mokado turned to him and said,

"Here's my offer. Work in my fish market for me and we'll give you the rent and twenty dollars a week. I need someone with a strong back to help me. I'm getting too old for this business."

Mieko was overwhelmed with Mr. Mokado's generosity. It had been a long time since anyone had shown any kindness to him.

"Thank you, sir," he said. In the next few hours he settled into his room and that night began working in the fish market.

Over the next six years, Mieko became the best employee the Mokados ever had. He worked from sunup to sundown, rarely socializing with anyone outside the shop.

Mieko continued to hate Americans, determined to avenge his family's deaths. When he went out at night, he could feel the hatred returning to him in the eyes of war veterans and people who had lost loved ones. He heard the hate daily, as Americans would harass the Japanese store owners and his other neighbors with bigoted remarks and gestures.

Mieko eventually took a second job to save more money. He knew he would have to be patient. It would take him several years to save enough money to fund his research. In the meantime he spent his spare hours at the public library reading everything he could find about viruses and weaponry. He also read magazines to learn about American culture.

In Japan, Tori's aunt had told them that America was a melting pot where people of any creed or culture could come and build a home. But now, the more he read the American magazines and newspapers, the more it became apparent to him that the United States was just a pot, not a melting pot.

At dinner one night in 1952, six years after he arrived in San Francisco, the twenty-six year old Mieko confronted Mr. Mokado with a question.

"Why do you live here and put up with all of the hatred from the Americans? What keeps you from moving back to Japan?"

Mr. Mokado smiled.

"Mieko, this country is different in many ways from Japan. I can run a business and have a vote in the government." He put down his fork. "This hatred you see is everywhere in the world, not just in America. Why did you come to America?"

Mieko avoided the question and turned and looked at Mrs. Mokado.

"A friend's aunt told me once that all cultures work together in America. But since I've been here it doesn't look at all that way. Throughout the country, each culture segregates itself, or is separate from the others. This has been the way since the founding of the country." Mieko turned back to Mr. Mokado. "Most of the cities have separate neighborhoods for European or Asian immigrants. Even immigrants from America's closest neighbor, Mexico, have their own neighborhoods."

"What's your point son? What did you expect?"

Mieko wasn't sure what his point was. He was just restless, not able to let go of the enduring grief and anger that visited him each morning. He could not forget his mission to kill a quarter of a million Americans. He would never forget the sights and sounds of a devastated Hiroshima.

"I'm not sure, sir. Excuse me." Mieko got up from the table and made his way upstairs to his room. He sat in the rocker near the window and looked down at the street crawling with Americans, all alive, all happy. He hated all of them.

One morning, two weeks later, Mieko drove down to the docks to pick up the day's catch. A sailor, still drunk from the night before, confronted him as he was making his way back to the truck. The two of them were in an alleyway hidden from view of the docks.

"Hey, Jap boy. Give me a cigarette." Mieko ignored the sailor and continued walking. "I said give me a cigarette." Mieko kept walking. The sailor jumped him and pulled a knife. "Don't ignore me you damn Nip."

As the sailor swung the knife Mieko grabbed his wrist and turned it back on him. The blade penetrated the sailor's rib cage and he fell motionless to the ground. He was dead. Mieko looked around. No one had seen them. Mieko dropped the knife through the dock into the bay waters. He walked quickly to his truck. He shook in fear as he drove back to the shop, realizing what would happen to him and the Mokados if anyone ever discovered the truth.

He knew he would have to leave San Francisco. His hatred for Americans had increased each day, and now he was a danger to those around him. He spoke with the shop owner that night.

"Mr. Mokado, you have treated me with kindness. I will never forget you and your wife. But I must leave."

"Where will you go?" Mr. Mokado asked.

"I'm not sure. I just can't stay in San Francisco."

"You've been a good worker for us Mieko, but I could tell the day you arrived that you had something else on your mind."

Mr. Mokado reached into his pocket and gave Mieko a fistful of money.

"Take this, son, and be careful. You are always welcome here."

"Thank you, sir."

He left the next morning. He knew that he needed to move away from the Japanese community where he lived since coming to the United States. He realized that someday his work would kill thousands of Americans, and he knew that if he stayed, he could endanger those around him.

So Mieko left the Mokados' home in San Francisco and drove east through the winding mountain roads of northern California passing town after town. He finally stopped in Sacramento. He found a small house for rent and moved in with hardly any belongings to his name. He got a job working the overnight shift in the maintenance department for a corrugated cardboard box manufacturer located at the edge of the city.

In the six years with the Mokados, Mieko had saved enough money working his second job to purchase the equipment he needed to start a small laboratory in his new home. Beakers, test tubes, refrigeration units, Bunsen burners, and a few expensive extraction machines filled his laboratory. For less than two-thousand dollars Mieko had everything he needed to grow the virus when he found it and kill a quarter-million Americans. Mieko was in the prime of his life and his mission was just beginning.

Mieko immediately set out to find the red-striped bees he worked with at Urakami prison. He made several trips to the Mojave Desert. On his first trip, after a long day of walking through the desert, Mieko set up camp. He spotted many plants and insects he'd never seen before, but he couldn't find the one bee with the red stripes. That night, as he began to crawl into his sleeping bag, he heard a faint hum. As he lifted the edges of the bag, the hum grew into a rattle. Mieko threw down the edge of the sleeping bag and used a cast iron griddle to beat the rattler in the bag. He killed it, spewing snake blood and organs all over the inside of the sleeping bag, leaving Mieko with nothing to sleep in for the night. It was the last time he would sleep outside of his car.

On his third trip he decided to explore areas closer to the mountain ranges. He found an area just south of the mountains, fed by a stream that seemed to magically appear out of the side of a foothill. A purple plant he'd never seen before grew in abundance there. Around its flowers he saw hundreds of the bees he needed. He caught several dozen and took them home.

Mieko's new home gave him a freedom to work on finding the solution to his final problem. He'd found the bees, rediscovered the virus, and now all he needed was a vehicle for distributing it into the public.

He did not know if he would ever find the answer, but Mieko was focused and patient. He studied hundreds of potential weapons. Most of them could not provide him with the scale of destruction he needed.

He found early in his research that his virus would not infect through the air, thus making any type of airborne detonation device useless.

He studied how he might poison a water supply, but he learned that American filtration plants were set up to keep such a disaster from happening on a large scale. He did find a way to access the water supply, but determined that at most he could have only killed five or ten thousand people before the detection systems discovered the problem.

For years Mieko wondered if his quest was in vain. After three years of searching, Mieko became frustrated and tired. He simply could not find the answer to his problem.

He devoted less time to his mission. Mieko found that the time passed quickly. His work in the factory kept him busy for ten to twelve hours every day.

In 1955 he was only twenty-nine years old, but he felt much older. He all but stopped looking for a solution to his weapon problem. Apathy and the everyday routine of his life lessened his anger and curbed his hatred. Most of all, his motivation to kill was thwarted by his inability to find a way to distribute the virus.

In January of that year he joined the rest of America and bought a television set. He watched it in the evenings when he wasn't working. On the evening of May 11th, Mieko was watching television when a program called "This Is Your Life" came on.

Like many of the shows of its time, it was performed completely live. Surprises were not uncommon. The show's format was simple. Ralph Edwards, the moderator, introduced a celebrity, and the remainder of the show featured key people from that celebrity's life. Some of the people appeared live on the show and others were heard via telephone.

This particular show Reverend Tanimoto, a Japanese minister, was featured for the work he had done to help the needy in postwar Hiroshima. One of the surprise guests that they brought in to meet Reverend Tanimoto was one of the pilots of the Enola Gay, Captain Robert Lewis. The Enola Gay was the plane that dropped the bomb on Hiroshima. The meeting created a lot of emotion in both gentlemen and Captain Lewis broke down in tears.

Mieko got a chance to see one of the men who dropped the bomb and killed his family. He felt a growing rage. The real surprise came when they brought out two women, victims of the atomic bombs.

Reverend Tanimoto brought them over to America to undergo plastic surgery to repair burn damage they had sustained from the bombs. They were two of twenty-five women that the news reporters referred to as "The Hiroshima Maidens."

Ralph Edwards only showed the women in silhouette so that they would not have to show their scars on TV. He then asked for donations that would go to help these women with their surgeries. The screen showed an address to send money:

Maidens
Box 200
New York 1, NY

Mieko jumped up from his chair, enraged when he saw how they were exploiting these women. He grabbed a pencil and hurriedly wrote down the address. He grabbed a sheet of paper and wrote his feelings.

"Dear Sirs,

I saw the actual damage in Hiroshima. My entire family was killed in the blast. Your exploitation of these women is reprehensible and is clearly propaganda in its worst form. No amount of skin repair can ever make up for the devastation created at Hiroshima and Nagasaki. God bless them all, but putting these women on display for all the world to see is a despicable attempt to show the world that America could fix the damage created by the bombs. Nothing could ever fix the damage.

Mieko did not sign the letter. He sent the letter the following day to Reverend Tanimoto at the address the program had indicated.

Over the next year little transpired to change Mieko's life outside of making a couple of new friends at his factory. He was always cautious about getting close to anyone for fear that they might become suspicious of his ultimate intentions. Fortunately for Mieko, in the late summer of 1955, three years after he moved to Sacramento, he met a couple of women at his factory. Both of the women were machine operators on third shift and usually worked on the same machine with Mieko. They provided him with some needed company.

But Mieko was still a loner at heart. He always remembered his vow to Tori that he would never love another. Sometimes, however, he felt like Tori's spirit was watching over him.

Mieko learned a lot about American prejudices from his experiences at the plant. There was a definite pecking order in the factory.

Eighteen white men made up the majority of the workforce on Mieko's shift. They let everyone else know who was in charge and routinely made life miserable for the rest of the workers. Mieko constantly dealt with it all. His supervisor was a newly-hired twenty five year old with little management experience. He was the only manager on the night shift, but because of his lack of experience, he had little control over any of the employees.

In addition to the white men, there were seven white women, three black men, three Hispanic men, eight black women, six Hispanic women, and the two new women, Carmen and Tsuki.

Mieko saw firsthand how cruel and insensitive the Americans were toward him and, especially, Tsuki. She'd recently moved from Japan to America to be with her sister. Tsuki had a severely disfigured face due to a childhood burn accident that she described one day. She told Mieko and Carmen her deformity was the result of a fire she had been caught in as a little girl in Kyoto, Japan.

The other workers, usually the adjusters, were cruel toward Tsuki and it incensed Mieko to new levels of hatred. Whenever Mieko heard a derogatory comment from one of the workers, he would remind himself of his ultimate goal to kill thousands of Americans.

"Someday," Mieko would tell himself, "they will all regret their cruelty." He would make sure of that. Whenever Mieko got mad, Tsuki would calm him down and talk about Japan.

Mieko put up with the abuse day in and day out.

One day, Mitch, one of the adjusters recently returned from a stint in the Korean War, shouted,

"Hey Jap, get the mess picked up around your machine. You're pulling all of our safety numbers down. We're all going to miss our bonuses because of you, stinkin' Nip."

Then Joe, a short, fat laborer chimed in.

"Did I see you looking at Doris earlier? Are you eyeballin' her? Don't be getting' any ideas, Jap boy. You touch one of our women and we'll kill you."

One time Tommy, the best adjuster on the shift, dumped coffee into Mieko's lunch pail, covering his lunch in cold coffee. Another time Neal put glue in the bottom of Mieko's locker. New forms of abuse were dreamed up every day. Mieko took it all. He knew he would have the last laugh.

That year, 1955, Mieko's search for his solution finally stalled out with no hope in sight. At times he thought of giving up his quest. He became less active in finding his final solution.

Like many Americans, Mieko settled into a daily routine that rarely changed. He adjusted to the bigotry that surrounded him and, like many people, began to believe that discrimination, bigotry, and hatred were just part of what we all had to live with to survive.

Chapter 12

In early May of 1955, Tori arrived in New York with twenty-four other women. In the few days that the Hiroshima Maidens had been together, an invisible bond of friendship developed among all of them. Tori developed a close relationship with Yoriko, a fifteen-year-old girl from Kyoto who was in Hiroshima visiting relatives when the bomb exploded.

Yoriko was burned across the back of her neck and around the left side of her face. The left side of her nose bent slightly due to her burns, but all of the right side of her face had been unharmed.

They sat next to each other on the plane ride from Japan. It was the first time either of them had been on an airplane. Both were extremely nervous. They kept each other company and shared stories of their youth to keep their minds off the flight. They spoke about the day of the bombing, but only briefly. It brought back too many sad memories for both of them.

"I had just arrived at our school," Yoriko said, "when my girlfriend, Yoshi, took me to a corner outside our building." Yoriko spoke so softly that sometimes Tori had a difficult time understanding her. "Yoshi started to tell me a secret about one of the boys in our class when the blast hit.

She was standing about two steps from the corner of the building and was completely exposed to the direction of the blast." Yoriko paused and swallowed. "I saw her skin erupt. It was hanging from her arms. She immediately passed out. I carried her to an aid station, but she died the next day." Yoriko paused and wiped a tear from her eye. "I was behind the corner, protected by the wall. It doesn't seem right that I should have lived." Yoriko looked down. "She was my best friend. She never even got to tell me the secret."

Yoriko shared stories of growing up in Kyoto. She was a quiet girl, but was delighted to have an opportunity to speak with anyone. Like so many of the *hibakusha,* Yoriko was so ostracized that she lived a lonely life, void of many of the everyday communications everyone else took for granted. That is why she so cherished her time with Tori. With each question that Tori would ask, Yoriko would reply with an answer that would last five minutes.

Although all of the Maidens were burn victims, Yoriko felt more sympathy for Tori than any of the others because of the extent of her facial damage. But Yoriko noticed that despite Tori's terrible misfortunes, she always seemed to be happier than anyone else on the trip. The two women stayed close during the entire trip.

On the second day after they reached New York they were given a short tour of the Statue of Liberty before being placed in the homes of Quaker families who had volunteered to house the Maidens while they recovered from their surgeries.

As Tori and Yoriko stood on the deck of the boat, gazing up at the statue, Yoriko spoke.

"Why would a country like this bomb us like they did?"

"Even great countries make mistakes, Yoriko," Tori replied. "This country has been kind to foreigners in the past. My aunt told us many stories of Americans who helped her family get settled when they moved here."

Yoriko turned to Tori.

"Do you think they are really going to be able to help us?"

Tori pulled her coat tight against the stiff spring breeze blowing across the cold waters.

"Yoriko, I believe many of them want desperately to help us. That, in itself, is what's important. I know they will try their best because our healing is their healing."

The next day it was announced that Yoriko and another one of the Maidens, Maki, would fly back to Los Angeles to appear on a television show featuring the man who brought them to the United States, Reverend Tanimoto. It was explained to the Maidens the importance of the show to raise additional funding for the surgeries. Millions of Americans would be watching.

That evening, Yoriko and Tori sat in the living room of the Quaker home that was hosting them. Suddenly, Yoriko had an idea.

"What if I can use this show to help find Mieko?" She asked Tori.

Tori wondered for a moment. She realized that Yoriko might be able to somehow get a message out that would help her find Mieko.

"What do you suggest?" Tori asked Yoriko. "What would you say?"

Yoriko was determined to help her friend.

"Tori, when it's my turn to speak I will simply ask if anyone knows of Mieko Takachi. I will ask them to send us any information they might have along with their donation. Someone must know him."

Tori grew hopeful.

"Thank you, Yoriko, I know it will work. God wants me to find Mieko."

She remembered the day she fell overboard. She still believed that God helped Mieko save her so that she could save him. She just did not know what it all meant.

Yoriko and Maki flew to Los Angeles two days later. Tori and the other Maidens gathered at a local church to watch the program. Tori anxiously waited for the moment when Yoriko would mention Mieko. The moment never arrived. When "This Is Your Life" aired on that May evening, neither Yoriko nor Maki were permitted to speak, except to answer a few direct questions from the host, Ralph Edwards.

The watching Maidens all wept as the show brought back vivid memories of Hiroshima that each of them wished to forget. Sadness mixed with anger.

"Why did the Americans do this? They have shamed all of us," one girl said. "It is bad enough we look like this, now everyone will look at us as freaks."

Another voiced her concern for the future.

"What if these surgeries don't work? What will we do then?"

As the program ended, Tori stared at the television, knowing that she had probably missed the best opportunity she would ever have of finding Mieko. In her short time in America, she better understood how vast the country was, and realized that finding Mieko would probably be impossible.

Yoriko returned from Los Angeles, apologetic and upset that she had not been able to help her friend. A week later Tori sat in a chair outside Reverend Tanimoto's office. The door was open and she could hear him as he prepared the schedules for the surgeries that were to take place later that month.

Tori had seen results from some of the first Maidens who had been through the plastic surgery. When the American doctors had seen the extent of Tori's burns, they privately told her that even their methods would not return her to normal. With this information, and little hope of finding Mieko, Tori decided to tell Reverend Tanimoto she no longer wanted the surgery. She wanted to go home to Hiroshima.

Tori visited Reverend Tanimoto's offices. She sat in the pale green waiting room. Plants of all sizes sat upon the shelves and tables. A framed copy of DaVinci's "The Last Supper" hung on one wall. On the other wall hung a brown cross woven out of sweet grass. While waiting to see Reverend Tanimoto, she said a prayer of thanks for all of the people who had been so kind to her on the trip to America. Then she heard the Reverend speak to his assistant. He seemed agitated.

"Here we are trying to help these young women and we get a letter from a man who claims we are exploiting them. Look at this letter from California. This writer claims his entire family was killed by the atomic bombs and finds it offensive that we are bringing these women here to ease America's conscience. And he doesn't even have the courage to sign his name."

"Reverend?" Tori had jumped from her chair and leaped into the office. "May I see that letter?" Reverend Tanimoto was startled, but handed the letter to Tori. She read the letter, noted the Sacramento postmark, and returned it. "It's Mieko, I know it's Mieko."

"Tori, you can't know that. Anyone could have written this letter."

"No, sir, not anyone. Only someone whose family was killed in Hiroshima, someone who lived to tell about it, someone who chose to come to the United States. It is Mieko, I know it."

"But Tori, the chances that the author is Mieko are very slim."

Tori insisted that God was leading her to him.

"I want to stay and find him. Will you help me?" She begged him.

The Reverend was concerned.

"You will have it rough. A 'Hiroshima Maiden' in America, alone. I don't know if you could make it on your own."

"Reverend, I have never been on my own, God has been by my side all along. He has brought me this far and He will help me find Mieko. Will you help me?"

"But what about your surgery?" He asked

"The surgeons do not think my operation will be much of a success. I will live without it. It never really mattered to me." She smiled at the Reverend. "We are what we are, we have what we have, and we do what we must do. I must find Mieko."

Reverend Tanimoto looked at Tori and knew she epitomized the faith he preached daily. He agreed to help her. With Reverend Tanimoto's help, Tori stayed in America and continued her search for Mieko when all of the other Maidens returned to Japan.

An airplane taking Yoriko and some of the Maidens back to Japan stopped in San Francisco in July of 1955. Tori hugged Yoriko, deplaned, and waved goodbye. She took a taxi to the bus station and took the first bus to Sacramento. When she arrived at the bus station in Sacramento, she went straight to a telephone booth and looked in the directory.

She was a twenty-eight year old disfigured Japanese woman, alone in a strange city. She should have been afraid, but her faith in God was unshakable. It was reinforced moments later as she thumbed through the telephone directory. A ray of sun broke through the bus station window and fell on the phone booth. Staring at her from the directory pages were Mieko's name, address, and phone number.

Tori smiled.

There have been few people who have ever experienced true joy like Tori experienced that day, in a phone booth at a bus station in Sacramento, California.

She bowed her head and said a prayer of thanks.

Chapter 13

Mieko had just finished lunch and was washing his dishes in the sink when the phone rang. It was probably another salesman. For most of his life in Sacramento, it seemed that only salesmen called Mieko. That is why he rarely answered the phone. But today he thought one of his supervisors might be calling about a special machine setup at the factory.

Mieko was now one of the best mechanics in the plant on third shift. He worked his way up to adjusting some of the most important machinery. Occasionally the supervisors from first shift would call Mieko at home during the day with questions about a machine setup or adjustment

"Hello?"

A weak female voice spoke to Mieko in Japanese. It was the first time he had heard his native language in years.

"Yes?" Mieko answered.

"Sir, I arrived in Sacramento yesterday from Japan with plans to live with my sister. But when I arrived, the landlady gave me a letter that my sister left for me. It said that she unexpectedly was forced to return to Japan with her husband to care for his sick parents. I have no one to turn to for help." Tori's heart began to race. "The landlady let me stay for the night on her sofa. But, she already rented out the apartment. I looked in the phone book to see if there were any other Japanese who I might be able to ask for assistance. You are the fourth person I have called. I need a job and a place to stay. Can you help me?"

Tori's voice wavered as she spoke. She prayed Mieko would not recognize her voice.

"What's your name?" Mieko asked.

"Tsuki Nakamura." Tori replied. Reverend Tanimoto had helped to arrange for Tori to carry a new name while in America.

"And where did you live in Japan?" Mieko asked.

"Kyoto," said Tori. She thought of all the stories Yoriko had told her of Kyoto, stories that would now represent Tsuki's childhood.

Mieko thought for a moment. His factory was looking for additional machine operators ever since a recent expansion. He decided to give Tori the phone number of the personnel department at the factory. He told her to talk to Mrs. Swift in personnel. He also told Tori that she could use his name as a reference.

"Tsuki, I think Mrs. Swift might know of some local apartments, if that's any help," he said. "Good luck. Maybe I'll see you in the factory sometime."

"Thank you, sir. I hope you are right." Tori hung up the phone and shook with excitement. She was going to see Mieko again.

But she stopped momentarily, thinking about what all this meant. She saw her reflection in the phone booth and began to cry. *"Mieko must never know who I am,"* she thought. *"I could never expect him to love me like this."*

She knew her hideous features drew only pity from everyone she met. She realized from that day forward, she could only ever be known as Tsuki, to Mieko and to everyone else.

When Tori called Mrs. Swift at the factory and used Mieko's name as a reference, she was told that she could begin work the following day.

Mrs. Swift told her that the factory was in desperate need of help and was glad to have received her call. She also referred Tori to an apartment complex that housed several of their workers.

When Tori arrived at the apartment complex that afternoon, with the factory's recommendation, the landlord balked at giving her an apartment. He did not mind renting to Orientals, but her freakish face scared him. He finally relented when he saw the Bible she was carrying. He was a Christian, too.

The next day Tori walked through Mrs. Swift's door to report for work. The office had three gray filing cabinets standing side-by-side, one with its drawer open, exposing the manila-colored personnel files of the plant employees. Mrs. Swift was pulling one of the files out of the drawer. Her back was to the door when Tori entered. Tori stepped into the office and looked down at Mrs. Swift's desk. She had over a dozen framed pictures of her children and grandchildren scattered about the desk.

Mrs. Swift turned, looked at Tori, and froze, initially shocked at what she saw. Pity shot through her. Pity to see anyone who had to endure life looking the way Tori did. Mrs. Swift fought to keep from staring at Tori's face, a face that was disfigured more than anything she had ever seen. But Tori's calm demeanor settled her. Tori diverted Mrs. Swift's attention by asking about the pictures on the desk.

"Is this your family?"

"Four sons and nineteen grandchildren." Mrs. Swift told her. "Always wanted a daughter, but it never worked out. That's okay. I've got plenty of granddaughters and another one on the way this December."

"Thank you for your recommendation yesterday." Tori said. "I was able to move into an apartment last night. And it's close to the plant."

Mrs. Swift then told Tori that she could start work that night on third shift. She thought it was wise to put her on a shift that would not be seen by many managers.

"So Mieko recommended you?" Mrs. Swift asked.

"Well, yes. He was kind enough to suggest that I should call you." Tori looked at the floor so Mrs. Swift would not have to look at her face.

"That Mieko is a strange one. Nobody can seem to get him to talk much. But he is one of the best machine adjusters we have." Mrs. Swift reached into a drawer. "Here Tsuki, take these brochures. They outline our benefit programs. Go home and get some sleep. If you've never worked third shift, you'll be surprised at how difficult it can be on your body to adjust."

Tori liked Mrs. Swift, but she almost laughed at the thought of how difficult third shift could be. She had lived through two atom bomb explosions.

Chapter 14

Tori arrived at the factory that night anxious and excited. She stood outside the doors, trying to get up the courage to walk in. It was a clear night, yet the smell of glue and ink mixed to create a noxious odor that hung in the air surrounding the plant. It made her slightly nauseous. She looked up at the green painted windows, a precaution taken during World War II to prevent the lights of the facility from becoming bombing targets for the Japanese. The factory was over fifty-years old, built around 1905 and used initially as an arms storage depot for the Army. It was a two-story building made primarily of red brick and built to withstand the test of time. In 1947 the owner purchased it from the government when they were closing many of the older defense facilities after WWII. He received a government loan and converted the building into a cardboard box manufacturing plant.

Another girl, attempting to get into the factory, walked up behind Tori.

"Excuse me, are you going in?" She said.

Tori turned and the girl saw her face. It startled her slightly, but she remained calm.

"Yes, I'm starting work tonight." Tori replied.

"Here? Really?" The girl introduced herself. "I'm Carmen, let me take you down and we'll find the supervisor."

They walked through the doors, down the steps into the basement where all of the heavy machinery was operating. Carmen took her to an office where three men were talking.

"Hey boss, new employee." Carmen announced.

The men turned and saw Tori. A quick expression of shock showed in their eyes as they looked quickly at one another. The supervisor, Don, motioned toward the door, and two of them exited.

"Thanks, Carmen." Don replied. "Your machine is just about ready to start. Mieko is making the final adjustments. Go ahead over. We'll see you in a few minutes." He turned to Tori. "You must be Tsuki." Mrs. Swift had told Don about Tori's face, so he was somewhat prepared when he met her.

"Yes, sir. I'm a good worker. You'll see." Tori replied.

"I'm sure you are." Don picked up his clipboard. "I heard from Mrs. Swift that you know Mieko, so we're going to have you train on his machine with Carmen, that girl who brought you in tonight. Do you know her, too?"

"Oh, no, sir. We just met outside the plant. But she seems very nice."

"Well, if you work out, we may keep you on their crew. They've been short a person for the past month. Follow me." Don led Tori through the plant.

The factory floor was covered in paper, dust, and dried ink. Machines with three-foot-long metal knives running at high speeds created noise that was deafening. The women operators frantically ran around their machines as cardboard boxes came off the line at high speeds and were put into containers for shipping. Adjusters stood by the machines, ready to fix anything. Tori and Don passed five machines and their crews as they made their way across the factory floor to Mieko's machine.

"Is that another Jap?" Tori heard someone ask.

"Hell if I can tell," another voice replied.

Mieko was busy adjusting his machine when the supervisor walked up behind him to introduce Tori. Eleven years had passed since their last meeting when Tori put the medallion into Mieko's hand.

"Mieko, hey, Mieko." Don yelled above the clanging of the machinery. Mieko could hear him, but continued to adjust his machine with his back to the group. "This is Tsuki, but I guess you know each other already. She's your new operator starting tonight. Carmen will help train her." Don turned to Tori. "Tsuki, you'll train under Carmen and Mieko on this machine. Mieko is one of our best adjusters, so pay attention when he asks you to do something. Our number-one priority is to keep these machines running at all times."

"Yes, sir. Thank you, sir." Tori replied.

Mieko thought he recognized her voice and turned from his machine to face the supervisor and Tori. He gasped slightly and fought to keep from staring at Tori's disfigured face. He did not recognize her.

Pity was what he felt. She saw it immediately. She had seen it hundreds of times from people she met over the past decade. Pity from anyone else was difficult enough. But pity from Mieko, the man she loved, washed out all hope she ever had of having him love her again. She resolved, once again, never to reveal her true identity to Mieko or anyone else. Mieko looked down at the ground and mumbled.

"Tsuki? Tsuki?" Mieko repeated her name trying to jog his memory and remember where they might have met. He realized if he knew her at all, it would have been before she suffered whatever fate had left her looking like this. "Do I know you?" He thought perhaps she had come from the Mokados' in San Francisco. He avoided looking her in the eye.

She could see that he was uneasy speaking with her, as most people were when confronted with her face for the first time. She tried to lessen his burden.

"I spoke with you yesterday on the phone about this job. You gave me Mrs. Swift's number. Remember?" She noticed his face had grown more mature. He was even more handsome than when she knew him in Hiroshima. She continued. "I want to thank you. I don't know what I would have done. Yesterday on the phone you said we might meet in the plant. You were right."

He remembered the phone conversation, but he never envisioned the voice on the other end to look like this. He'd seen burns like this in Hiroshima, but not nearly as severe. He wanted to ask her how she'd been burned, but he realized that was not appropriate.

Tori saw he was growing more uncomfortable. She turned toward Carmen, who had been watching the conversation and recognized that Tori was trying to ease Mieko's discomfort.

Carmen was smiling when Tori turned to ask her a question.

"Is this machine difficult to work?"

"Not at all. Let's look over the daily shift reports first and then we can look at the operator's manual. We always have to cover all the rules in the manual for training, but you'll probably just ignore most of them, like the rest of us. Have you ever worked in a factory?"

Carmen slid a copy of the daily report onto a clipboard. Mieko turned and went back to adjusting the machine.

"No, I've only worked in hospitals." Tori replied.

"Hospitals? Well, I don't know how you'll use any of that experience around here. Not to say there aren't a lot of sick individuals around here, but I'm afraid most of them are beyond any cure. Especially the adjusters." She adjusted her blouse. "Most of them are pigs. They'll do anything just to get a peek down your shirt. They're pretty disgusting, except for Mieko. He's the only decent one among them. And maybe Gary, but he's pretty crude, too."

Tori laughed at Carmen's manner. Carmen grabbed a pen and showed Tori the form they had to fill out at the end of each shift.

The two women went about their duties, and for the next eight hours Tori stood by quietly and trained with the young eighteen year old. The two of them packed the freshly-made cartons into shipping containers while Mieko ran around and made whatever adjustments were necessary to keep the machine running.

Over the next week Carmen noticed several times how Tori smiled whenever she looked at Mieko. On the fifth night, just before lunch, Carmen asked Tori.

"Tsuki, you like him, don't you?"

"Like who?" Tori replied.

"Like who? Well, Mieko, of course. You smile like a Cheshire cat every time he comes by us."

"No, I don't think so." Tori said, feigning ignorance. "What's a Cheshire cat, anyway?" Tori realized she needed to get control of her emotions or she might be found out. She gave Carmen a serious look. "I am just grateful to have a job, and Mieko was kind enough to help me find it. I have realized my dream of coming to America and living. That is what I'm really smiling about."

"Whatever you say, Tsuki," Carmen laughed, "but I think you've got a case on that guy."

"No, not at all." Tori thought quickly. "In fact, I have a boyfriend who is coming over to America soon to meet me. We are to be married next year."

"Really?" Carmen replied. She didn't believe Tori for a minute. She could not imagine that Tori had any suitors. But the answer sparked Carmen's curiosity. She tried to call Tori's bluff. "So is your fiancé short or tall?"

Tori paused and the lunch siren blasted. She avoided the question as everyone scattered for the next half hour to eat lunch.

During lunch in the factory everyone broke into separate groups. The white men and women took over the largest tables at the center of the small lunchroom. They controlled the only radio in the lunchroom. The black and Hispanic women sat at the smaller tables in the far corner of the lunchroom. The black men usually congregated around the maintenance crib. The Hispanic men hung around the gum vats. Mieko always ate alone at his machine.

Most of the third-shift workers were hard-working folks, making just enough money to live day-to-day. Life's frustrations would reveal themselves during lunch in the form of friendly verbal abuse poured out on each other. More often than not, the women were the butt of sexist jokes. People would laugh, as if the jokes were humorous, but most of the time, the jokes were simply crude.

Joe was typical.

"Yo, Peggy. How do you turn a fox into an elephant?"

Peggy shrugged.

"I don't know."

"Marry her." Joe replied cackling.

Gary was an exception. Still single and immune from the daily pressures of married life, he always kept the girls laughing, but with less cutting humor.

"Hey Sheila," Gary yelled out. "What do you call a woman who knows where her husband is every night?"

Sheila bit.

"Okay, give it to me."

"A widow."

Gary kept the shift laughing at lunch. He even made Carmen laugh. She thought he was cute.

94

But from the first night, Carmen avoided taking Tori into the lunchroom. She knew what would happen. Tori's face would make her the brunt of every joke. Carmen had already overheard cruel remarks from Mitch and Neal about Tori.

For the first month, Carmen and Tori ate lunch outside whenever they could. Carmen had a favorite saying.

"The twinkling stars are angels in the night sky and do not care about the color of your skin, or from which country you come."

Tori would look up at them and think about her family.

Carmen and Tori became close friends. Carmen was the only American who looked past Tori's deformities and saw the gentle soul that existed beneath. The others in the plant kept their distance, mostly because Carmen and Tori were not part of any clique.

Carmen, although she looked Latino, had mixed blood, and neither the Hispanics nor the blacks ever took her into their groups. She had dropped out of high school the previous year and started working on the third shift after applying at three other factories in the area. Her father died in the war and her mother was forced to work to raise Carmen and her three brothers. Carmen, the oldest sibling, saw how difficult it was for her mother. She decided to quit school, get a job, and help out with the bills. She worked at night, slept in the morning, and took care of her brothers when they got home from school. She never had a sister.

Carmen never did believe Tori's story about a boyfriend coming to America. Carmen only saw a lonely woman who needed a companion.

During that first month, Carmen recognized the kindness in Tori's heart. She was certain that, over time, Mieko would see it, too. Carmen decided she would do whatever it took to help build a friendship between Tori and Mieko. She knew Tori's face would prevent anything romantic from occurring, but she felt that these two lonely souls might find some comfort in each other's company.

One night in the second month of Tori's employment, Carmen decided to take Tori and eat lunch near Mieko's machine.

"Mieko, do you mind if we eat over here? The lunchroom is always crowded." Carmen asked.

"I don't usually see you go into the lunchroom." Mieko said, noting the peculiarity of her request. "But you can eat wherever you want."

He actually was glad to finally have some company. For several years he had been the only "Jap" in the factory. He came to realize that none of the other employees would take the step to befriend him for fear of being ostracized by their own groups. He knew many of the adjusters were bigots at heart, and he was an easy target. However, his skill as a machinist was unmatched by any of the other adjusters on the shift, a fact that kept him employed through tougher times.

Mieko never cared to make friends with anyone. On many nights, Carmen and Don, the supervisor, would be the only people Mieko would speak to the entire shift. That was fine with Mieko. He focused on his own personal mission, to develop the virus as a weapon. Friendships were not important to him. In time though, he found it to be a lonely existence. That first night Carmen and Tori had lunch with Mieko started what would be a ritual that would last for many more years.

Most nights Carmen spoke and Mieko and Tori would listen. Fortunately for them, Carmen was one of those rare individuals who was always upbeat and could remember the latest jokes and trivial gossip. She would keep the conversation, or monologue, as it often became, moving along all the way through the lunch break.

"Tsuki, did you see the dress Betty had on last night?" She said, laughing, "Oh, my gosh. I wonder what she did with the rest of the curtains."

The two Japanese did not understand all of her American humor at first, but Mieko was simply glad to have company, and Tori was glad to be near Mieko.

"Mieko, do they play baseball in Japan?" Carmen asked one night. "I love baseball. My old boyfriend used to play baseball. He played shortstop. Do you know what a shortstop is? He's the most important player on the field. Did you know that?" Tori would just smile as Carmen talked on and on. "Why are these machines always so filthy? Why don't they get some people in here and clean them up. I'm not going to clean my machine. I don't get paid enough to work on the machine and clean it, too."

When Tori did speak, she would tell of her childhood in Kyoto and how she worked in the hospitals during the war. She seldom spoke of her burn injuries. Once, when pressed to explain her injuries, she made up a lie and said that she had been trapped in a burning shed when she was a small girl and was saved by a boy who lived next door.

Mieko was always interested when Tori spoke of her hospital experiences. Some of the patients she described reminded him of people he had worked with in Hiroshima. Mieko seldom spoke, but Tori would occasionally ask him strangely specific questions about growing up, and he would have rushes of memories he had long forgotten.

Tori was as happy as she could ever expect to be. She got to be by Mieko's side every day. Almost all of her prayers had been answered.

One warm summer night, when Carmen called in sick, Tori found herself alone at lunch talking with Mieko. They walked outside and stood under the full moon.

"Mieko, have you ever had a girlfriend?"

Mieko was not one to speak openly, but her question brought back a vision of Tori handing him the medallion on the day he left Hiroshima.

"Yes, when I was young."

"What was she like?"

Mieko looked up at the moon.

"She was . . ." he hesitated, picturing her flowing hair, "beautiful." A tear rolled down his cheek.

Tori saw his profile against the moonlight. She wanted so badly to tell him. But she knew it could never be the same as it was on those mornings at the harbor in Hiroshima.

"Where is she now?"

It became too painful for him to talk about her.

"We stopped seeing each other years ago." He conjured up an excuse and turned to go back into the plant. "I almost forgot. I've got to get back and work on the next machine setup. I'll see you later." That was the most he ever said about Tori.

Over the next several years Mieko, Tori, and Carmen became the closest of friends at work. Like so many work relationships in America, they never socialized or even saw each other outside of the plant. Mieko's plan for revenge became less meaningful to him. A general apathy set in, life held little change, and conflicts in the plant maintained a status quo except on three days every year.

On Pearl Harbor Day, Mieko could sense the hatred from many of the other employees for many years after the war. The feelings usually lingered for just a day or two before everything returned to normal. On the anniversaries of Hiroshima and Nagasaki, he and Tori would see newspaper and television coverage of the tragic events, all covered from an American perspective, always stating the necessity of the bomb to end the war, never condemning those individuals who decided to focus the power of nuclear devastation on thousands of innocent civilian families instead of the soldiers at war.

Mieko gave up temporarily trying to find the weapon to dispense his virus. His hatred became dormant, like a cancer in remission. The 1960s brought the Kennedy assassination, the Beatles, hippies, and the Vietnam War, all fodder for conversation as time passed quickly in the factory. The only things that changed within the factory walls were the pastel colors on the restroom walls and the rock music blaring on the lunchroom radio.

Tori lived as Tsuki from Kyoto, able to keep her true identity concealed. Only occasionally would she talk about the war.

Most notably, there was one instance in the summer of 1971. Carmen, thirty-three years old and feeling the squeeze of the hands of time, announced that she and Gary were going to be married. The two of them had danced around marriage for several years, but the time had finally come and Carmen wanted to start a family.

In the midst of lunch the night of her announcement, Carmen spoke seriously to Mieko and Tori.

"You know, Gary's father died during the war fighting the Japanese and he has never been able to get over it. He blames all the Japanese." Carmen looked at the floor apologetically. "He told me he can never be friends with a . . . a Jap. I'm sorry, I'm sorry. I hate to even say that word, that's what Gary says. He doesn't even want me to eat lunch with you. I don't know what to do. You are both such good friends."

Mieko completely understood. He looked to Carmen.

"The war created a lot of hatred. There is nothing you can do to change that." Mieko knew from his own feelings why Gary felt the way he did.

But Tori spoke up.

"You are wrong, Mieko. We must all fight, every day, to change the hatred around us. Both sides in a war are on the wrong side. There is no right side. Peace is the only right side," she continued. "Our emperors and presidents are the ones who decide to go to war. It's not me or you or our fathers or mothers who have any say in the matters of war. Yet, who gets killed?" She spoke faster. "It is always the innocent who shed their blood, the simple people who just want to raise their families and get by. They get slaughtered and killed, for what? So some emperor can claim to have more land in his control?" Tori was almost shaking with anger. "We do not make the wars, but it is imperative that we make it our responsibility to keep the peace. There are far too many orphans in the world because of leaders who can't keep the peace. Everyone must learn to forgive and move on." Tori spoke in earnest. "Don't you see? We must all move beyond our religious and political differences, beyond the colors of our skins and the warped ideas of supremacy that almost all groups of people cling to in one form or another."

When Tori finished she looked up to see Mieko and Carmen staring at her. They had never seen Tori so angry and animated. "I'm sorry," she said, "but it's all true. The hatred must stop with us."

Carmen spoke with Gary that night and told him what Tori had said. Gary was unaffected.

"I just wish they would stay in their own country where they belong." He said. "Why do they have to come to America and take all of our jobs?"

"Gary," Carmen said, with a dose of anger in her voice, "Tsuki and Mieko are my friends, just about my only friends. You don't have to eat lunch with us, but I will continue to eat with my friends, just as I have for the past fifteen years. If you don't want to marry me because of that, so be it."

"All right, all right." Gary backed down. "Don't make a federal case out of it. Eat lunch with them if it's that important to you. Just don't include me."

At times it was difficult, but Carmen loved Gary. She loved his laughter and his usual gentle manner. She understood his attitude and why he felt the way he did about the Japanese, but she didn't agree with it. After all, she had lost her father in the war, too. But she recognized we all deal with things in our own way. His one prejudice toward the Japanese would be the one fault of Gary's that she would have to live with. They drove to Reno the next week and got married.

100

Through the 1970s, life in the factory resembled that of a typical small community. In 1972 Carmen had her first child, a beautiful girl. Also on a snowy night of that same year, two of the older adjusters died in a car wreck on the way to work. They were replaced with two veterans of the Vietnam War. In 1975 Sheila, the Mark IV operator, was found out to be a lesbian and quit the following week. She couldn't stand the harassment from the adjusters. In 1976 Danny announced his intentions to go into the ministry (a plan that lasted six months after which he returned to the plant, losing his seniority on the adjusters' wage ladder).

The most important event of the 1970s for Tori occurred one evening when she was relating a story to Carmen and Mieko. She was describing events at the hospital she worked at in Nagasaki and told the story of Misako, the little six-year-old girl who had died in the bombing. She told them how the girl had touched her face and asked her if her own face had suffered the same fate. Within the story Tori divulged the fact that she had been burned at Nagasaki. When it happened, Tori immediately realized what she'd revealed and did not say another word that night.

Carmen and Mieko saw what they thought was embarrassment and did not ask her anything else about it. It was obviously a secret she had been trying to hide. She never mentioned it again. After many months Tori thought it was forgotten. However, after hearing Tori's story, Mieko thought she must also secretly share his hatred for Americans. Even after all of her speeches about peace and forgiveness, Mieko was so blinded by his hatred that he felt Tori must hate the Americans who changed her life so dramatically for the worse.

The 1970s were ending, and even though the owners were able to keep most of the people working throughout the decade, the economy was going downhill and so was the company. Change was in the wind.

In 1978, the family who owned Mieko's company since its founding fell on hard times. The founder had died in 1973 and the remaining sons were incompetent, never able to coordinate their efforts to make a substantial profit. In late 1979, the sons met with a large conglomerate that was buying up and consolidating all types of paper, stationery, and printing companies.

This new company would buy several small companies in a region, consolidate them under one roof, and fire the redundant employees. The consolidation would usually combine workforces, which oftentimes resulted in labor and cultural clashes.

This merger would prove no different. It came as a surprise to all of the employees. A company meeting was held late on a Friday afternoon before the Memorial Day weekend. The founder's oldest son, the current president of the company, addressed the employees.

"My father built this business with the help of many of you and your fathers. My family owes a debt of gratitude to you all. However, times are changing. We can't compete as a small company in this business anymore. And for that reason we've decided to sell the company."

The employees were stunned.

"Are we all fired?" Several people asked.

"No, no. Over the course of the next few weeks the new management will decide who will be asked to stay on. Many of you will be keeping your jobs. For the rest of you, on behalf of my family, we thank you for your years of service and my brothers and I promise we will do everything we can to make sure you get a fair severance package."

One anonymous voice yelled from the crowd.

"Bullcrap!"

A cackling of lesser "bullcraps" followed.

After the holiday, the new management came in and released half of the employees. Everyone received four weeks of pay for severance. Most of the highly-paid adjusters were let go. Because of his high efficiency ratings over the years, Mieko and his crew, Carmen and Tori, were asked to stay. When management asked Mieko if there were any other adjusters worth keeping, he put in a good word for both Gary and Tommy. He knew Tommy was a great adjuster, but he recommended Gary because he didn't want to see Carmen working without her husband. The new management kept both of them. No one ever told Gary how he kept his job.

Later that month they brought in machinery and employees from another plant they had closed. More announcements were made to those remaining employees that business was changing.

"Profit margins in cardboard boxes have eroded over the years, folks," the plant manager said. "This plant is now going to start producing all types of stationery. We're going to be the biggest supplier in the country within three years."

The employees had heard all of the "company speak" before. They didn't care what they were manufacturing; they were just happy to have jobs.

The new supervisor on Mieko's shift, Tim, heard of Mieko's superior mechanical abilities and assigned him to one of the more difficult machines.

"Mieko, I'll need you and your crew on the new RA machine. We have another one being delivered next month and we'll need you to train Gary on it." Tim turned to Gary. In his short time on the job Tim recognized Gary's skills were not to Mieko's level. "You got any problems with that?"

"No, sir. Not at all." Gary found this turn of events insulting and degrading. He had to report to the "Jap." He would have quit, but he and Carmen had a family now and they had three more mouths to feed.

Tim continued, sharp and to the point.

"There will be a special training session tomorrow night. Be there." He walked away.

The first week with the new consolidated crews from the other factories was not pleasant. No one wanted to work together, and there were a lot of bad feelings about new workers replacing old friends. Quarrelling increased. The minorities took more verbal abuse than ever before.

In particular, Mieko noticed how, after all these years, Tori, once again, was forced to endure all of the slurs and comments from the new workers that had long been said and forgotten with her former co-workers.

"Freak."

"Burn Baby."

"Human Torch."

The slurs seemed more mean-spirited than ever before, possibly displaced anger from a workforce unsure of their own future. It didn't matter why. Mieko's hatred for these people was reignited.

He didn't know what he would do until the technical support agent from the machine manufacturer began giving his crew instructions about their new machine. The technical agent began his training session. He was from Nashville and sounded like it.

"I'd like to welcome y'all to this here training session. I'm gonna show y'all how this company plans to stay in business. Forget everything ya know about your old machines, because they ain't never comin' back. Take a look at your new breadwinner." The technician unveiled the new machine brought in from their closed factory. "Ladies and gentleman, welcome to the world of envelopes. From now on, your lives will center on creating the best envelopes in the world. That's right, envelopes. Everybody uses them, and the industry is growing twenty percent a year."

"But we don't know anything about envelopes." Gary said.

"You will." The technician glanced at Gary, and then looked directly at Mieko, as if to challenge his reputed machine abilities. "This here machine *should* be able to run somewheres around a quarter million envelopes per eight-hour shift. Some of the best adjusters in our Tennessee facility can make it scream up to 350,000 envelopes a shift." He paused for reaction from the group. "Our goal is to get our envelopes into every household in America, and I'm here to show all of you how to do it. Any questions?"

When the technician said the words, *quarter million* and *every household in America*, Mieko's mind clicked back to a day when a truck driver told him how many people they initially thought had died in Hiroshima and Nagasaki. His thoughts raced back to those days after he returned to Hiroshima and saw the results of the bomb.

Mieko's adrenaline rushed through his body with a sudden realization. His knees became shaky for an instant and he needed to lean against the machine to catch his balance. Tori, standing across the room, always keeping an eye on Mieko, noticed his reaction.

Mieko had spent years searching for a vehicle to distribute his virus. On this night, the weapon he had sought for so many years was delivered to him.

"A quarter million?" Mieko asked.

The technician looked squarely at Mieko, convinced he'd effectively challenged him and smiled.

"Hell, no offense, but your kind can probably make 'em run faster with all your transistors and stuff." Some of the newer workers laughed. Tori felt bad for Mieko, but inside his head, Mieko was already planning his revenge.

A quarter million.

After twenty-five years Mieko had finally found his weapon. Mieko could now even the score. In one shift he could produce enough envelopes to kill a quarter of a million Americans.

I t took Mieko only two weeks to get his laboratory up and running again. Tori noticed that Mieko seemed to be energized and thought it was something to do with his new job.

Mieko stopped having lunch with Tori and Carmen. He was too busy. He was constantly exploring the best way he could find to infect the glue that was put onto the envelopes.

Tori noticed the change in Mieko. She became concerned and spoke to him before they started the shift one night.

"Mieko, why aren't you at lunch these days? Did I do something wrong?

"You, Tsuki? No, no, I just started reading how I should have more hobbies. I figured I was boring you and Carmen with all of my usual stories. I'm just taking a little break. Probably start up again in a week or so."

Tori walked away, not completely believing him, but happy to have spoken with him about it.

Mieko's research continued. He frequented the library during the days. Mieko learned about direct marketing. Billions of envelopes get used every year, but many of them are sealed by machinery, or not sealed at all. If a book club sent out a million solicitations with return envelopes enclosed, they could only expect to receive two to five per cent in responses. That meant for every million envelopes mailed, at least 950,000 envelopes got thrown away by consumers who didn't join the club. More importantly to Mieko, it meant that only 50,000 people would lick the envelopes. He needed to find a way to infect over a quarter million that would get licked.

Mieko learned more about the virus and his machine. He discovered that the virus carried in the bees would survive the heating lamps on the machines if he turned the temperature down. But this, in turn, forced him to run the machine at a slower speed to ensure the glue would cure properly. It meant he needed to work a double shift to hit his goal of a quarter million envelopes. More importantly, he would have to come up with a reason for having a slower production run. This would not be easy because Tim, the new supervisor, was constantly checking machine efficiencies and Mieko rarely ran slower than the machine standards dictated.

He finalized his plan. On the night he would contaminate the envelopes, his first step would be to mix the virus with the seal glue. This would be easy, because all of the machines contained open troughs called glue boxes. These boxes held the glues that were applied to the envelopes and later licked by the consumers. Part of Mieko's responsibility as a machine adjuster was to keep the glue boxes on the machines full of glue. He would have complete control over the contents of his machine's glue box.

Secondly, Mieko needed to make sure he infected only envelopes that were sure to get licked. That meant he had to select the right group of envelopes to contaminate. His new machine ran billing return envelopes for one of America's largest credit card issuers. Every credit card customer paid his monthly bill by sending in a check in the return envelope. Most customers lick the envelope before returning it with their payment. Mieko would use the virus on the night they were running those orders.

Finally, he planned to work a double shift and infect up to three hundred thousand envelopes. Because of the workload and his seniority, he could almost always work a double shift when he wanted to. His plan was set.

On a Wednesday in September of 1980, Mieko decided he needed to run just one test in order to gauge the proper concentration of virus needed to infect the seal glue. That afternoon Mieko prepared a potent sampling size of the virus and placed it into a larger half-gallon jug of a concentrate that would blend with the glue without changing its color. He had to make sure the glue maintained its usual color. Colorings of the glues were grounds for stopping a machine run. It usually meant there was a poor concentration level of adhesive in the glue formula. Sometimes rats would find their way into the larger glue vats and drown, coloring the glue with their blood, which forced machine shutdowns. Other times flies, roaches, or other flying insects would land in the glue boxes, discoloring the glue further. He put the jug in his lunch pail and carried it to work.

That evening, at the beginning of his shift, he looked at the schedule. His machine was scheduled to run 100,000 envelopes for the National Rifle Association immediately following lunch. They were to be used for membership renewals.

Mieko spent his lunch break setting up the run. He asked Carmen and Tori to get an extra batch of cartons, a task that took them away from the machine for about twenty minutes.

Everyone else in the plant was on lunch break. He put on a special pair of gloves and went over and took the jug out of his lunch pail. He nervously walked up to the glue boxes at the machine and started to take the lid off of the jug. He was about to pour it into the glue box when a voice spoke up.

"Hey, Mieko, is Carmen around?" Gary had suddenly come around the corner of the machine and up from behind him. "What's in the jug?" Gary asked. "And what's with the gloves?"

Mieko turned quickly to Gary and searched for an answer.

"Just some new glue stabilizer I've been trying. It hasn't worked very well. I'll let you know if I find some that does."

"Glue stabilizer?" Asked Gary. "What's that do?"

"I'd really like to explain, but . . . ."

At that moment Jack, the third-shift foreman stepped into view and interrupted before Mieko could finish answering Gary.

"Mieko, the Sup wants to see you right away. He's upstairs in the office. Said it was something about your overtime request. What's with the gloves?"

"That's what I asked him." Gary said as he walked back over to his own machine.

Mieko ignored them and went to the office. He had almost been caught. He could not afford to take another chance. He would have to forget about a test and go right to a major production run.

Mieko placed the jug under his bench and went up to the supervisor's office on the third floor. When he returned, he took the jug home.

A month later Mieko planned to infect the seal glue of over 300,000 envelopes of a major credit card issuer. The run of envelopes was for several million and would last for at least two days, so Mieko was able to plan ahead of the shift. The victims would be as faceless to him as the victims of Hiroshima and Nagasaki were to all of America over thirty-five years earlier.

But now, at the age of fifty-four, even though he finally developed his plan, he felt a strong need to tell someone his story, to share his victory. He wanted to share how he had waited for so long and was finally going to extract revenge for Japan. There was only one person who could understand, only one other person he was sure hated the Americans as much as he did.

The afternoon before he intended to infect the envelopes, he stopped by Tori's apartment. It was the first time he ever visited her apartment.

Tori still lived in the one-bedroom apartment she had moved into the day she arrived in Sacramento. Ownership of the building had changed hands several times, but no one ever asked her to leave. Mieko looked at the mailboxes out front of the building and saw that her apartment was number six on the third floor. He made his way up the creaky stairwell. Across the dark hallway a door cracked open and a female neighbor peered out at Mieko. The door closed and he heard the locks being turned. He made his way to Tori's door and knocked.

Tori was watching an old movie from her small collection of videotapes. Earlier that year she had purchased a video camera and VCR machine so that she could film the songbirds in the park. It was a new technology, and one of the few extravagances she'd ever spent her money to buy. But she'd become an avid birdwatcher in the past ten years, and the camera allowed her to capture the beauty of the birds she had come to admire. The VCR machine also allowed her to tape her favorite old movies from the television. She'd built a small collection, mostly musicals and comedies that reminded her of the days in Hiroshima when she and her sisters would perform for each other. She was wearing an old tattered robe and fuzzy slippers when she answered the door.

"May I come in?" Mieko asked, alarming Tori with his presence.

"What are you here for? Is everything OK? Is something wrong with Carmen?" She couldn't understand why he was visiting her for the first time in twenty-five years.

"No, nothing is wrong. In fact everything is perfect. That's why I want to talk to you." Mieko made his way into the room. "Can we talk for a few minutes? I have something important to tell you."

"Mieko, you're not sick, are you?" She couldn't believe he was standing in her apartment.

"No, no, nothing like that."

She suddenly realized what she was wearing. "Let me go change." Tori said. "Have a seat, I'll be right out."

Mieko looked around the apartment. Framed watercolors of harbor scenes and birds hung throughout the apartment. On the table, next to her armchair, was a small glass vase with three white roses sitting next to a carved wooden jewelry box. A Bible lay on the table, opened to chapter five of the Book of Matthew.

Tori came back in three minutes, dressed in an emerald green silk kimono with yellow and white birds embroidered on the sleeves. Her slippers were made of white silk. She sat in the chair across from Mieko.

"Would you like some tea?" she asked picking up the teapot.

"Please." Mieko replied. "These pictures, did you paint them?"

"Yes, I've taken classes over at the community center for years." Tori poured two cups of tea.

"They seem so familiar." Mieko stared at one of the harbor paintings. Tori noticed and spoke to divert his attention.

"Why are you here Mieko?"

He looked back at Tori.

"We've known each other for a long time, since you moved here, when was it?"

"1955." Tori's memory quickly flashed back to her trip with the Maidens. It made her smile.

"Tsuki, since 1955 we've had lunch together thousands of times. In all that time I never really told you why I moved to America. Were you ever curious?" Mieko sipped his tea.

"Well, Mieko, we all have some secrets we keep to ourselves. Like a woman's age, you never ask." She smiled again thinking how pleasant it was to have Mieko sitting in her apartment.

"Well, I'd like to tell you. I came here shortly after the war. A war that killed my entire family and everyone I loved." Mieko set his cup down, stood up, and made his way over to the window overlooking the park. "Tsuki, the Americans bombed Hiroshima, my city. They destroyed all of it. Everyone I knew and loved died that day. And our Emperor gave up." He turned to face her. "I didn't give up." Mieko decided to tell her outright. "Tsuki, I came to this country for revenge."

"Mieko, why are you telling me this?" Tori asked.

"Because I know you must share the same hatred. Look what they did to you. You told us yourself that your burns were from the bombing in Nagasaki." Mieko paused. "I'm going to get revenge for all of us. I'm going to kill one person for every person who died in Hiroshima and Nagasaki. And no one can stop me. I have the perfect plan. I'm going to infect the envelopes and I'm doing it tonight."

Tori was shocked. She had never seen this dark side of Mieko. She became nauseous.

"Dear God," thought Tori, *"I have been so happy for so long just being able to live near Mieko, that I have failed to see his pain and suffering."*

She suddenly realized that she was the only person who could save Mieko and hundreds of thousands of Americans.

She thought as fast as she could. She stood up to face him.

"Mieko, you mustn't do this. It isn't right. This will not bring back any of those who died."

"But Tsuki, you must feel the same way. Look what they did to you. How can you not hate these Americans?" He backed away from her. "You were there and saw with your own eyes what happened. You must hate them."

"Yes, I was there, Mieko. You were not. This was what happened to me." Tori said pointing to her scars. "I saw thousands of people left homeless. I helped mothers and fathers die as peacefully as possible, knowing that they would never see their children grow old. I saw pain that should never be seen again. My entire family was killed." She stepped closer to him. "But Mieko, I learned that forgiveness saves your soul and lets you live for the future. I cannot change what happened then, but I can change what will happen. I will not let you do this thing. It will kill innocent people, just as the bombs did in Hiroshima and Nagasaki. You will become like the men you hate. I can't let that happen to you. I love you too much."

Mieko looked away.

They had never talked about love, but both of them had felt a closeness develop over the years. He knew deep down that he had developed some type of love for her, but he had a responsibility to his family to keep the oath of revenge he had made years before. When he thought of loving Tsuki, he felt a sense of guilt as he remembered the oath he made to Tori years before.

"I'm sorry, Tsuki. I am not the man you think I am. You do not know what I have been through. I must fulfill my promise to my family." He thought for a moment. "I do have feelings for you, Tsuki, but years ago I made a vow to someone that I would never love anyone else. I'm sorry. I have nothing I can give you."

Tori began to cry. She was afraid of what she might have to do. She walked over to the table and opened the wooden box.

"Mieko, years ago, in a Hiroshima hospital, I met a woman who convinced me that we must live for the future. Before she died, she gave me this medallion of hope and told me to always look for the good in people. I know you have lost much, but you are a good man. You take it now and think about the future. What good will come of your killing thousands of Americans? No one in Japan will care. In fact it is a stronger country today than it has ever been. No one is asking you to forget the past, just forgive."

Tori put the medallion into Mieko's hand.

Mieko stared at the samurai and the sun. He had not seen it since the day he had traded it to the harbormaster years ago. His heart began to race.

"Tsuki, do you remember the woman's name who gave you the medallion?" He anxiously asked.

"Yes, her name was Tori." Tori said.

Mieko froze. He had never mentioned Tori's name to anyone.

"What else do you know about her?" He demanded.

Tori thought quickly.

"She was one of the patients I met years ago in a Hiroshima hospital a few months after the bombing. She was sick and dying. She told me that we must all forgive and go on. That is why I believe as I do."

Mieko looked more closely at the medallion and wondered how Tori had ever recovered it from the harbormaster. He suddenly realized something he'd never known. Tori must have been alive when he had returned to Hiroshima.

"But how could she have gotten the medallion if she was confined to a hospital?" He muttered.

Mieko was growing confused. The confusion fueled his anger. He suddenly remembered his mission. He turned back to Tori.

"Tsuki, if Tori was dying when you knew her, it must have been from the radioactive fallout. Now, more than ever, I must make all of America pay." He made his way toward the door.

Her ruse hadn't worked. Tori knew what she had to do next.

As Mieko walked out the door, Tori began to whistle. He stopped dead still when he heard the sound. It was a sound that brought back a memory of Kusatsu Harbor. He saw Tori standing by the boulders at sunrise. The wind was blowing her hair and she was laughing. Laughing at Mieko's attempt to be a musician.

Tori was whistling "The Harbor Song," the tune Mieko had created just for her. Mieko turned to face her.

"Did Tori teach you that song?"

She looked at the floor. She didn't know what else she could do. Mieko spoke louder.

"Did Tori teach you that song?" His anger was exposed in his raised voice.

She looked him in the eye, and with tears streaming down her face she stammered.

"No, Mieko, I . . ."

"What, what, you what?" He yelled at her in frustration.

"I . . . I . . . am . . . Tori."

He slowly moved closer to her and stared into her eyes, looking through her tears and past her burns. He gasped as he brought his hand up to his mouth. Suddenly he saw what his hatred had prevented him from seeing for over twenty-five years.

"It is you." He embraced her, and in between his tears of joy, he showered her with kisses, as he whispered repeatedly, "I have missed you so much . . . missed you so much."

"I know." She whispered back. A smile came to her lips as she suddenly realized that all of her prayers had been answered. "But now Mieko, you must forgive them, all of them."

He looked around the room at the three roses and the watercolors. It all made sense to him now. They sat on Tori's sofa for hours talking about their journeys from Hiroshima to America. Then, Mieko took Tori into the bedroom and they fell asleep in each other's arms, something both had dreamed of for many years.

When morning finally came, they resolved to put the past behind them and move back home to Hiroshima.

In the days that followed, Mieko destroyed all of the virus he had developed and burned all of his research papers. He wanted to make sure no one else ever discovered the virus. He and Tori both gave their notice and left their jobs two weeks later. He told everyone he was having heart problems and needed to retire. They surprised Carmen with their announcement.

"We're going home to Japan to be married. We want to see if we can adopt some children and raise a family."

"You're getting married?" Carmen was overflowing with joy for the two of them. "But how did you decide so fast?"

"So fast? We've worked together for twenty-five years. We just decided it was time." Tori told her. "We hope you can come and visit us in Japan. You'll always be welcome in our home."

Tori feared Carmen would feel like she had been deceived all those years, so they never told her the true story. To all of the other workers in the plant they were just two lonely foreigners going home to Japan. But both of them wanted their story to be told. Before they left, they used Tori's video camera to film their story over an old copy of *The Sound of Music* which Tori had previously taped on her VCR. They had no idea who would find it or if it would ever be found, but the two of them decided they would leave it in God's hands.

On the day they left for Japan, Carmen drove them to the airport. She walked them to their gate.

"Tsuki, I'll always remember our lunches together." Carmen said wiping a tear from her eye. "May God be with you and Mieko."

Tori embraced Carmen.

"Come visit us any time. Our home will always be open to you and Gary and your beautiful daughters." Tori reached into her purse. "This has meant a lot to Mieko and me. We want you to have it now." Tori handed Carmen the medallion. "Thank you for your friendship over the years. I do not know how I would have survived without you. I'll write to you when we get settled." Tori kissed her on the cheek. "Goodbye my friend."

Carmen felt like she had lost her only sister.

On that night in 1981, as my wife and I watched the tape Mieko had made, his narration ended with Tori coming out from behind the camera and sitting next to him. Tori had been behind the camera the entire time. She spoke quietly and only had only one thing to say.

"We must all learn to forgive one another."

That is where Tori and Mieko's story ends. But that is not the end of our story.

Chapter 19

OUR STORY

After the tape ended, my wife and I sat silently for several minutes. I looked over and saw that she was crying. The story Mieko had told us on that videotape seemed unbelievable.

It would have seemed the work of a delirious old man to almost anyone else who would have stumbled onto it.

However, my wife, Carmen, and I were not just anyone else. I was the one who discovered that videotape on that fateful day in January, 1981.

That videotape showed Carmen and me the real story of Mieko and Tori. We'd worked beside them for years and never knew any of it.

For years, Carmen had felt it was her matchmaking that had gotten this lonely couple together. That night on the videotape we learned that much greater forces had been at work, the same forces that put that videotape into our hands.

I also knew I needed to tell Carmen what I'd done, something that changed our lives forever.

"Carmen, I was always jealous of the way Mieko could make the machines run. Mieko wouldn't admit it, but I always believed that he developed some tricks to make his machine run faster." I swallowed hard.

"I suspected that the gum stabilizer I caught him using one night was the secret to his being able to run his machine so fast. I was convinced that Japs always had some kind of secrets. I couldn't accept the fact that Mieko was simply a better mechanic than me. I was so sure that the gum stabilizer must be his secret that I decided to take some of it."

"Gary, you what? How?" Carmen fingered the medallion that now hung around her neck.

"I stole half of his bottle of gum stabilizer on that night last September when he planned to run the first test to infect the NRA envelopes. I saw him place it under the bench when he was called away to talk to the supervisor. I filled it back up with water and mixed it so he wouldn't notice anything was missing."

"What did you do with it?" Carmen asked.

"Well, the first time I used it was in late November, the week after Mieko and Tori left for Japan. I remember the envelopes were for renewal notices for that gay men's magazine we always ran envelopes for. Anyone renewing a subscription had to lick the seal to send in their payment. It was a run of about two hundred thousand envelopes."

"But nothing happened, nobody died, did they?" Carmen looked at me with a look of shock in her eyes that I'd never seen before.

"Not that I know of, but that's not all there is."

"There's more?" She was still reeling from having seen the story on the videotape. She could barely believe me.

"A couple of weeks after that the plant closed down the third shift because business was so slow. Remember when they transferred us to first shift? Well, it was on first shift that I used the rest of the stabilizer. I think it was our second day. I used it on the return envelope for that huge credit card company job we ran for days at a time. I must have infected thousands of the payment return envelopes."

"Gary, how could you do this?"

"Carmen, I didn't know. I just thought it would make the machine run faster. Besides, I didn't have a lot of the stabilizer left at that point. I don't know how many envelopes became infected. The run was for over five million envelopes, but I know the stabilizer didn't last the entire run because my glue box ran low midway through the shift. It may have infected a few hundred thousand or a few million. There is no way of ever knowing for sure."

"Oh, my God, Gary. What are we going to do?"

"Let's just sit and wait. Maybe nothing happened. Maybe that stuff wasn't really dangerous."

"But you saw what Mieko said on the tape."

"I know. Let's just wait and see what happens."

Nothing did happen for several months, but then it started.

Three months after we watched the video, in March of 1981, the newspapers reported the occurrence of a rare disease, developing predominantly among the gay population. The symptoms were everything Mieko had described, a complete breakdown in the immune system.

The fact that this disease hit the gay population, before any other group, prompted all types of speculation about its origin. News reports of 'the gay plague' filled the newspapers and tabloids. The media acted as if the disease was only connected to the gay community.

While our ignorant co-workers joked about the gay population finally meeting with their just rewards, my wife and I firmly believed that my contaminating those envelopes was the real cause of the outbreak. America's homophobia grew with each new report of the frightening new disease labeled as AIDS. I saw innocent people being persecuted and I couldn't do anything about it. I did not have any answers to the problem and feared I could be convicted of a crime if I told the truth.

For the first time in my life I saw prejudice from another perspective. It made me acutely aware of my own shortcomings and made me face my own unresolved issues of grief over my father's death.

I finally came to realize that I couldn't blame the Japanese people for my father's death. Certainly he died at their hands, but my father really died as a result of war that evolved from prejudice and hatred. Prejudice and hatred that is so widespread that on average, over thirty major conflicts are in progress every day of every month of every year around this small planet.

Unfortunately these events also took a toll on our marriage starting at the end of 1982. More reports of AIDS deaths filled the newspapers that year and Carmen grew distant from me for a few months, not sure of what kind of man she had married. I worked hard to assure her that I was still a loving husband, a good father, and an honest man. But all she could think about were the people I might have killed.

She would go days without speaking to me. With Mieko and Tori gone, Carmen found two new lunch buddies on first shift, Kathy and Roger. Kathy was a divorced grandmother of four and operated a machine next to Carmen's. Roger was the plant electrician. Five years earlier his wife and daughter had died in their sleep from smoke inhalation in a fire caused by faulty electrical wiring. Roger had been at the plant the night of their deaths, rewiring one of the machines. He always blamed himself for their deaths since he'd put in all the wiring in his home when it was built.

Both Kathy and Roger were from the company we had merged with. They would occasionally meet with Carmen after work for drinks. One night Carmen was so angry with me that she stayed out all night. In the morning I confronted her at the front door.

"Where have you been all night?"

"I stayed with Kathy. I'm thinking about divorce."

"Divorce?" I was stunned.

It was a wake-up call I needed. I loved and needed Carmen. I wanted desperately to work things out and get our family back to where it was before I had infected the envelopes. She sat down with me that week and we had a heart-to-heart talk. I told her how much I needed her and she told me how much she loved me. I tried to convince her that it wasn't entirely my fault, but I knew it was.

We agreed to stay together. We still loved each other. We knew we needed to get stronger for each other and our children. Life got better after that night. We began to spend our lunches alone together.

However, AIDS eventually spread to the general population, as we feared it would. Everyone has to pay his credit card bill sometime.

Two years after we viewed Mieko's videotape we decided to destroy it. We never went to the police. What could we have told them? What if they decided to take our daughters away from us? We could not risk that happening.

After all, it was my fault that this disease was released into the public. That's what I believed, although there is no way to prove it now. In any case, it changed our lives. For many years, my wife and I worked alongside Mieko and Tori. I always thought that they moved to America to escape their own homeland and take from us what was rightfully ours.

I was so ignorant and prejudiced. Looking at how I lived and how others viewed the AIDS crisis solidified my understanding that ignorance lies at the root of most prejudice.

On our anniversary two months ago, we received a greeting card from Tori. As I opened it, a picture fell out. Tori enclosed a photo taken months earlier of her, Mieko, and their three adopted daughters, standing and smiling by the boulders at Kusatsu Harbor.

On the back of the photo Tori wrote,

"Sunrise on Kusatsu Harbor"

The note she enclosed brought both good and bad news.

First, she happily told us of how her oldest daughter decided to pursue a life of nursing. Then she told us that Mieko, at age 63, succumbed to lung cancer one month earlier, probably as a result of his years of smoking at the factory. Any secrets regarding a cure for the virus were now buried with him.

Tori went on to speak of her other two children and their plans for the future. In her words you could feel her faith. This woman who had known more terror and despair than any of us could ever imagine continued to keep her hope for the future. Her letter concluded with,

"Visit us anytime. My girls and I will take you down to the harbor where we walk each morning. We go there often and pray. It is the most beautiful place on earth.

All our love,
Tsuki"

Tori changed our lives for the better and I'll always believe saved my soul. We never told Mieko and Tori that we discovered the videotape or that I stole the stabilizer. We agreed that they had seen enough tragedy in their lives. We felt they deserved to live out their lives in peace.

As for Carmen and me, we both worked on the machine and, as adjusters and operators do during their workdays, we personally tested those envelopes, unaware that what I had put in the glue was a virus, not a stabilizer. After seeing that videotape in 1981 we realized what might happen to us.

Through 1982 and 1983 we read how the spread of AIDS was unstoppable. For several years we denied that it could happen to us. Finally in 1984, after feeling some symptoms, we were both tested and found to be HIV positive. We don't know if any other employees tested positive, but no one ever connected the problem to the factory.

The fact that Carmen and I contracted the disease, confirmed what we had always suspected. My actions with the stabilizer must have released this dreaded disease into the world. How else could we have contracted it?

Five years have passed now and it is 1989. I've been involved with the church. I pray a lot.

I never really considered myself a prejudiced man. I guess most of us don't. In these last four years, Carmen and I have come to appreciate life and our daughters more than ever before. We have lived each day gratefully acknowledging our ability to live and love together. Now, my doctors tell me, I probably have only a year or two to live.

Last month Carmen, my beautiful wife, and mother of our children, died from complications due to AIDS. That is one of the reasons why I am writing this story now.

Carmen had every right to hate me. We both believed it was my prejudice that had caused me to steal Mieko's virus and unleash the disease that killed her. But Carmen, my angel, my sweet, sweet angel, took Tori's words to heart and forgave me.

The night before she passed away, Carmen handed me the medallion. She made one final request and then she smiled and whispered to me. "Gary, please promise me that you'll help our daughters to always look for the sunrise and learn the lesson Tori taught us all."

She squeezed my hand one last time and said,

"We must all learn to forgive one another."

Did I tell you I have always loved my wife?

Chapter 20

I t was two weeks after Carmen passed away that I was packing for
a trip when a letter arrived at our home. It was addressed to Carmen and marked "Confidential." There was no return address on
the outside. It was marked in red ink with several corrections written
to the address. The original address showed an incorrect zip code. The
postmark was over two years old, which meant it had been lost at the
post office for quite some time.

I opened the yellowed envelope and took out a sheet of lined note-
book paper with handwriting in pencil that looked to have been written
by an unsteady hand. It was from Roger, the electrician. We hadn't seen
him since he left the plant for another job in early 1983, shortly after
Carmen and I resolved our marital problems. I began reading.

December 2, 1986

Dear Carmen,

I hope this letter finds you well and in good spirits. I miss our lunches together. I miss you. I wish you hadn't settled your issues with Gary just after we started to bond. I'll always wish we'd met under different circumstances, but our one night together, even as inebriated as we were, has always been a fond memory for me.

However, that's not why I'm writing this letter.

I hate to tell you this, but a year after I left the plant, in late 1984, I found out I was HIV positive at a routine physical. I never felt any symptoms and for about two years I was in denial. This October it escalated into full blown AIDS. I think it's God's way of punishing me for what happened to my wife and daughter.

A few months ago I ran into a former acquaintance who had contracted HIV before we met in early 1982, which means I was probably infected when you and I spent the night together. I am so sorry to have to tell you this, but I suggest you go and get tested as soon as possible.

I would have written sooner, but I have been living in a shell since I found out, fighting to face the truth and inevitability of it all. I probably will not be around for too much longer (the doctors say two to four months). I pray that I did not infect you. Please, please forgive me for putting you in this position, but I did not know.

Love,

Roger

Our perspective of life changes daily as events unfold around us. Some we can control, others we cannot. Roger's letter made me realize that I may not have been responsible for all of those deaths. Maybe the virus I released had nothing to do with AIDS. Maybe I didn't even release a virus. What I do know is that my prejudice set into motion a chain of events that resulted in Carmen's death. My actions drove her into another man's arms. One way or another, it was my fault that my wife died.

Most of us do things in life that we regret. I've done my share, but I've also worked hard to be a loving husband and a caring father. Few of us live our lives without fault. You may think it's a coincidence that we found that videotape, but Carmen used to tell me that there are no coincidences. I believe her now.

I finished packing and took my daughters to the airport. We boarded the plane to fulfill Carmen's last request. Tori greeted us at the Hiroshima airport and we introduced our daughters to one another. I continued to call Tori by the name she chose in America, Tsuki. Her girls thought it was a nickname we had given her.

We drove back to their house and our daughters talked to one another all evening, with Tori acting as a translator. Early the next morning we all walked down to the refuge that Mieko had spoken of on that videotape. It was as beautiful as Carmen and I had imagined.

As I stood at the harbor I could envision the many stories Mieko shared with us on the videotape. I envisioned Mieko and Tori coming to the refuge each morning when they were teenagers. I saw Mieko bidding farewell to a tearful Tori as he left for Urakami Prison. I saw remnants of the old harbormaster's shed where the medallion had been exchanged.

I envisioned Tori being blown into the water when the bomb exploded and, then standing at the dock months later, unknowingly watching Mieko's boat sail away to San Francisco. My eyes began to water. I remembered the final photograph she sent us of their family standing at the harbor.

I remembered the other reason I came on the trip. There was some unfinished business. I took Tori aside.

"Tsuki, I was so wrong to treat you and Mieko the way I did for all those years. Words can't express how truly sorry I am for how I behaved. Could you find it in your heart to forgive this ignorant old man? It would mean so much to me if you could."

Tori took my hand and smiled.

"Gary, we both forgave you long ago."

I turned her hand over and opened it.

"Carmen loved you like a sister. She wanted you to have this." I placed the medallion into her hand.

"Thank you." She pressed it to her chest. "I loved her, too." A tear came to her eye. I'll never forget her smile as she opened her hand to view the medallion one more time. I looked at it and saw something I'd never seen before. The figure on the medallion no longer resembled a robed samurai with a bow. It looked like a robed angel with wings.

To fulfill Carmen's last request, we returned to our daughters on the docks. We all stood facing the harbor waters. As we joined hands and bowed our heads, the sun began to appear over the dark waters in the distance. In just a few seconds, blazing streaks of bright yellow-orange light streamed out across the blue horizon like fingers reaching to heaven. Tori led us in a prayer.

"Dear God, bless this soul. Take her into your arms, this mother, this wife, this friend. Love her, keep her, and protect her until we can join with you and her in your kingdom. Amen."

I opened the urn and a sudden gust of warm wind blew up. We felt her presence and knew Carmen's spirit was there with us as we spread her ashes over the water. We stood in silence as the waters reflected the brilliance of the morning sun and we watched as the waves carried her away with the outgoing tide.

A gull appeared from behind us, flying directly over our heads and out toward the horizon. We watched in silence as it disappeared into the morning light.

I whispered goodbye, and for the first time in my life I saw the sunrise on Kusatsu Harbor.

The End

REFERENCES

1. *Nine who survived Hiroshima and Nagasaki:* Personal experiences of nine men who lived through the atomic bombings, Robert Trumbull, Dutton, 1957.
2. *The Hiroshima Maidens,* Rodney Barker, Viking 1985.
3. *Nagasaki 1945,* Tatsuichiro Akizuki, 1981.
4. *The Widows of Hiroshima,* Edited by Mikio Kanda, translated by Taeko Midorikawa, St. Martins Press, 1982.
5. *The Day Man Lost,* Compiled by The Pacific War Research Society Kodansha International, Ltd., 1972.
6. *Children of the A-Bomb,* Compiled by Dr. Arata Osada, translated by Jean Dan and Ruth Sieben-Morgan, Peter Owen Ltd., 1959.
7. *The Bells of Nagasaki,* Kodansha International, 1984.
8. *Hiroshima,* Victoria Sherrow, MacMillan 1994.
9. *The Atomic Bomb, Voices from Hiroshima and Nagasaki,* Editors: Kyoko and Mark Selden, M.E. Sharpe Inc, 1989 p.173–190.

EPILOGUE

Terror comes in many forms, sometimes by the hand of man, sometimes by the hand of nature.

Over twenty-five million people worldwide have died from AIDS since 1981, with over three million dying in 2005. Over forty million people are currently living with the HIV virus, with almost five million newly infected each year. A recent U.N. study predicts that by the year 2010, the average life span in African regions affected by the epidemic will drop to forty-five years from a high of fifty-nine in the early 1990s.

As we all work to eradicate terrorism throughout the world, let us all work together to find a solution to the AIDS epidemic, a terror that is killing thousands each day worldwide.

Just as importantly, let us also work together to clear the earth of nuclear weapons. We all must work to ensure that there will be no more Hiroshimas or Nagasakis for our children, grandchildren, and the world.

—D.D. Maloney

To order additional copies of

S U N R I S E
O N
KUSATSU HARBOR

Have your credit card ready and call

Toll free: (877) 421-READ (7323)

or order online at: www.winepressbooks.com